THE WITCHES' KITCHEN

THE WITCHES' KITCHEN

Allen Williams

L B

LITTLE, BROWN AND COMPANY
New York   Boston

Little, Brown and Company

Hachette Book Group
237 Park Avenue, New York, NY 10017
Visit our website at www.lb-teens.com

Little, Brown and Company is a division of Hachette Book Group, Inc.
The Little, Brown name and logo are trademarks of Hachette Book Group, Inc.

First Edition: October 2010

The characters and events portrayed in this book are fictitious.
Any similarity to real persons, living or dead, is coincidental and
not intended by the author.

Library of Congress Cataloging-in-Publication Data
Williams, Allen, 1965–
The witches' kitchen / written and illustrated by Allen Williams. –1st ed.
p. cm.
Summary: When Toad wakes up dangling over a bubbling witches'
cauldron with no memory of her former life, she just manages to escape
and, with the help of an imp, a fairy, and some other friends, she sets
out to discover her identity.
ISBN 978-0-7595-2912-0
[1. Toads–Fiction. 2. Magic–Fiction. 3. Identity–Fiction. 4. Fantasy.]
I. Title.
PZ7.W65581Wi 2010   [Fic]–dc22   2009045625

10   9   8   7   6   5   4   3   2   1

RRD-C

Printed in the United States of America

To Duncan, who makes bad things good.
To Maeve, who makes old things new.
And to Victoria, who makes sense.

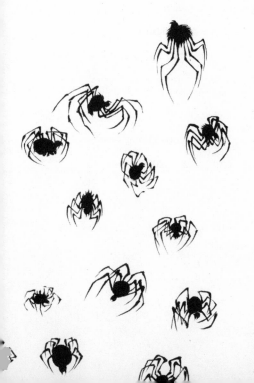

Deep in the walls of the keep, the vast Kitchen lay in darkness. But it was not still nor had it ever been. Magic infused the Kitchen, rippling through it, changing everything that lay within, causing it to constantly move and surge like a living beast. It was a world of unending chaos where the very walls and foundations shifted without warning. Fixtures were not fixed and it was quite possible that one might see a herd of cupboards marching about minding their own business. It didn't quite exist in our universe, but butted up next to it—parallel, touching, but not overlapping. The Kitchen belonged to two witch sisters, who had been around for a very, very long time. They had discovered it and bent it to their own evil recipes. The Kitchen had been around before the Sisters and likely would exist long after their demise.

Things live in the Kitchen. Some are good...most are not. It is a feral place of hard life and harsh survival. The gentle and the kind do not fare well there as a rule, with but a few exceptions.

The Kitchen was dark...and eternal but not still...

CHAPTER ONE

Give her to me." The voice sliced through the silence like a carving knife, and in the total darkness Sarafina imagined her sister's thin, outstretched hands, grasping, expecting to be obeyed.

Though they were standing face-to-face, nearly nose-to-nose, Sarafina could only just perceive Emilina's gaunt silhouette as a glow slowly began to emerge from the depths of an ancient cauldron squatting a few feet away.

A book lay spread open on the table nearest Emilina. She would frequently glance at it as if she were reading, but the anemic light did not brighten its pages at all. In fact, the light bent around the book as if afraid of what was written there. Here in the Witches' Kitchen, the light wasn't welcome. The foul, creeping things that dwelled here did not enjoy the light. The darkness kept their secrets.

Sarafina obeyed her sister, extracting a small, bloated body from a red velvet sack with her thick, rough fingers. A huge, hulking woman, possessing incredible strength, Sarafina had pale, pink-mottled skin that hosted patches of dark brown freckles across her cheeks and nose.

"Still unconscious? Good. But she'll wake soon enough, yes, she will," Emilina murmured. *"Step lively, pot."* Tall and as angular as a grave digger's spade, she considered herself an expert in the crafting of bitter sorrows. Her hair was long, black, and as rigid as piano wire.

The cauldron's four grotesque legs began to move on cloven hooves. Like a frightened, wounded horse, clipping and clopping in an uneven rhythm, the cauldron lurched to the Sisters' side and lowered itself, shivering, into a crouch without spilling any of its contents.

Sarafina paused, glancing at the small body held tightly

in her meaty fist as she handed it to her sister. Reaching up, she fidgeted with the pearl necklace stretched tightly around her thick neck.

Emilina glanced up, surprised at the sound of soft clicking in the dead silence. By the growing cauldron light, she saw the small skeleton of a bird perched atop Sarafina's rounded left shoulder. In one eye socket it had a single, raven black eye. The other was empty.

It stared back at Emilina, paused, and clicked its beak again.

"Sister," Emilina said drily, "did we not agree to destroy all of the disobedient cribs? Are we now wearing them as jewelry?"

The lines of Sarafina's perpetual scowl now deepened as her eyes sparked a fleeting expression of anger. "It's not jewelry," she said with the slightest hint of defiance. "I'm going to experiment on it. I have to see what went wrong with this batch. After that, the crines can have it for all I care."

"Ahh," Emilina drew the word out, mocking her sister. "Right. Well, have your fun then." She paused, and then added, "It's of no consequence to me."

Most of the time, most things are exactly as they appear. The thing Emilina was so closely examining *appeared* to be a toad, and it was starting to wake up.

The first thing the Toad saw when she opened her eyes was a cadaverous pool of green, bubbling slime. Tendrils of putrid steam uncoiled toward her. She stared at it in confusion.

She was dangling upside down over a huge seething cauldron, held aloft as if she were a wishbone by two very odd-looking women, each pinching a hind foot. They whispered to each other and though the Toad could hear them quite plainly, she couldn't understand the language they spoke. She knew witches when she saw them.

This was not a place she wanted to be.

She wriggled, but she couldn't budge her legs an inch. Her bizarre captors were oblivious to her. Now quiet, the women stared at each other, slowly leaning closer and closer together, until it looked like their faces were blurring or . . . melting toward each other.

The Toad only tore her eyes away from the horrific sight when movement appeared nearby. A terrible walking bird skeleton crept up toward the rotund woman's neck. The little creature turned and looked at the Toad with its one shiny black eye. Then it did something quite unexpected.

The crib pecked. Hard.

Sarafina squealed as the needle-sharp beak of the crib punctured the soft flesh of her neck. Her face snapped back away from Emilina's as the skeletal bird struck again and again. As Sarafina reeled, frantically swatting at the creature, a tiny rivulet of blood began to trickle down the front of her dress. At last, her hand found the crib and batted it off her shoulder into the darkness as the string of pearls snapped with a pop.

Instinctively, she began snatching at the orbs of her necklace that were cascading down to the floor. She managed to capture a single large pearl; and as she raised it in her doughy fist triumphantly, her left foot unfortunately found another one. She pitched forward, her head smashing viciously into the bridge of Emilina's nose with a resounding *crack*.

Emilina landed pinned under her sister's weight, unable to draw even a shallow breath. The cauldron spun for a moment trying to catch its balance before it tipped up on its edge, legs kicking spastically in the air. Its contents rapidly splashed across the stone floor. Its light extinguished.

Sarafina began to roll her ponderous weight off the uncomfortable lump beneath her. Finally able to inhale, Emilina sat bolt upright and issued a sound like a reverse scream. The air whistled into the vacuum of her lungs and as the darkness closed in around her and became complete, she shrieked...

"Where in the bloody blazes is the Toad?!"

CHAPTER TWO

he Toad in question was dangling from a chain some fifteen feet above a floor that she couldn't see.

Her situation hadn't greatly improved. She was still hanging upside down. When the wide witch had smashed into the thin one, the Toad was thrown in a high arc and she'd landed on a thick chain dangling in the deep blackness of the room. Her left leg was firmly wedged in an iron link all the way up to the middle of her thigh.

With effort she twisted and looked up. Toads normally have excellent night vision, but in this unnatural darkness, she could only make out a few inches of the chain. But her movement jerked the chain ever so slightly. Just as the chain made a solitary *clink,* she realized how quiet the room had grown.

She froze in a panic. *Did they hear?* she wondered. She listened, petrified, but there was nothing but silence from below. She couldn't be sure this was a good thing, though. Just as she thought she couldn't stand it anymore, she discovered something else to be afraid of.

The chain was moving. And this time it wasn't her.

"Sister," Emilina began in a muffled whisper. She had one hand clasped over her broken, bleeding nose. "You brought the candles, yes?" She somehow managed a tone that was both civil and menacing.

"Why would I bring candles? We never use candles! We always use the cauldron!" Sarafina said defensively.

"Ahh, so it is. You are right. We don't have time to trifle with preparations when there are broken cribs to play with."

Sarafina started to argue but Emilina cut her off coldly. "We shall seal the room and bind it. Then we shall gather the proper tools and come back in a few hours. There is nowhere for her to go."

"Do you have the Book?" Sarafina asked hesitantly.

"Of course I have it. Do you think me so dull that I couldn't find that book, even in the dark?"

"No, I was just..." Sarafina began, then said in a low whisper, "It can't be left alone."

"Collect yourself, Sister. I must attend to my...injury. I

would prefer to keep the rest of my blood inside my body."

Sarafina turned toward what she thought was the front of the room and took a step. Her hip sharply clipped the edge of a table and there was the sound of breaking glass as something fell to the floor.

"It's moved again," Sarafina said. "The room has changed."

"As it has always done," Emilina said, the calm, dry evenness returning to her voice. "Here, take my hand. I will lead you."

Sarafina clasped her sister's hand. It was wet.

"And, Sarafina, when we come back..." Emilina paused. "Bring the candles."

The chain was moving. It was a subtle swaying, back and forth, as if something were climbing up or down, hand over hand, or worse: claw over claw. The Toad wanted to flee but she had no idea which direction to go, because she couldn't tell if the movement was coming from above or below her. She looked down and could see nothing. Straining her eyes, she could only manage to see seven or eight inches down the chain.

This is insufferable, she thought. Abruptly, the swaying stopped. In the silence she heard a click, then a creak, and very far away she saw a thin sliver of yellow that began to widen.

The Witches stood in the frame of a very large double door. The Toad squinted against the sudden brightness from the hall beyond. Their silhouettes were a thin line of black and a mountain of shadow.

They're leaving! she thought as she watched them quickly pass through the opening and shut the door. She could hear it being bolted from the outside.

With the Witches gone she decided that she would risk trying to right herself again. She reached one pebbled green hand to the link above her trapped leg, pulled herself nearly upright—and came face-to-face with a single shining black eye. An eye that was sitting in a skull that ended in a very wicked beak, and on the beak there was blood.

She screamed. Or at least, she tried to scream, but what came out instead was a huge, belchlike

Croooaaak.

The bird-thing clicked its beak once and that was all it took.

Toads have excellent survival skills in the wild. They are very adept at escaping things that want to devour them. The problem is that they usually escape by jumping, which is exactly what this toad did. She couldn't stop herself. She let loose a ferocious kick, which freed her trapped leg. One second she was clutching a massive black chain, the next

second she was hurtling sideways
through the darkness.

She had just enough time to
think to herself, *Brilliant, absolutely
brilliant!*

Then she began to fall.

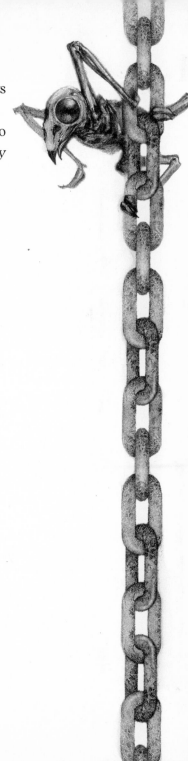

CHAPTER THREE

t's an unusual feeling, falling into complete darkness, and if the distance is great enough, it feels like flying...until you hit the ground.

The Toad lay on her back, motionless. She was groggy, her head ached, and her body hurt all over. She felt awful. Her arms and legs tingled as if sharp pointy things were pressing against her skin from all directions. If she tried to move even a little bit, the feeling intensified into actual pain.

"Don't struggle like that," a whispered voice came from above her, and she froze, her sudden fear forcing her foggy brain into clarity. The words sounded threatening. "If you struggle, you're just going to get hurt."

The Toad exclaimed, "What do you want?"

"If you don't want my help, just say so, but just so you know, the pinfetcher that built this little monstrosity is going to come back. It won't be happy to find you in its nest, and if there's an egg down there . . . it's going to hurt you, badly."

The Toad tried to glance around, straining her night vision to its limits. In the dull gleam of a thousand tiny angular lines she saw a roundish shape a few inches from her head.

That is an egg, she thought, *whatever's up there is right about that. And those are real pins. I don't want to know what builds a nest out of needles.*

"What should I do?" she said in a croaked whisper.

There was a moment of silence and then she heard: "Hey, big fella. Ohh. I guess you're a girl, aren't you?"

There was a strange, guttural sound that slurred into a rolling growl. She was pretty sure it wasn't coming from her rescuer.

"Whoa! Whooaaa! Look at what I have," the voice said. "Look how shiny and pointy. It's just for you. Catch!" There was a loud thump and then the sound of something shuffling away on leathery footpads.

"Quick," he returned, "hold up your foreleg. When I grab it, completely relax your body."

She lifted her right arm straight up into the air, sucking in her breath as she scraped against a bundle of needles. It felt like her forearm was being crushed as an immense hand closed around it.

"That's easy for you to say." She took a deep breath and exhaled. As she did, she was surprised to be able to release some of the knotted tension in her small form.

In one fluid motion the hand lifted her straight up and drew her from the insane nest. But instead of putting her on her feet, he tucked her under the crook of his arm as she felt him take long strides away from the nest. She still couldn't see him.

After a moment she said, "Put me down." In spite of the fact that he had saved her from one peril, the Toad certainly didn't want to go from the frying pan to the fire. Or, as it were, the needle nest to the dinner plate.

"Yes, yes," her benefactor said, "but we have to move farther away. The pinfetcher won't pay us any notice if we aren't close to its nest."

He walked for a few brief moments before she was set on her feet. They kept moving and the Toad stayed close enough to bump against the leg of her new acquaintance with each hop she took. Eventually they stopped, and she was squatting on the stone floor looking up at the relentless darkness.

She was too overwhelmed to speak. The Toad still couldn't see her savior at all but finally she managed, "How much longer till morning?"

"Morning! Ha, I haven't seen morning in years. The sun never rises in the Kitchen."

"What, you don't mean to say that it's always this dark, do you?" she asked nervously.

He began to answer but she interrupted, "Wait, what kind of a kitchen? Who are you?"

"I am Nathaniel Jackard Heartswallow. My traveling companions, when I decide to travel in company, call me Natterjack. Pleased to meet you," he said formally.

"What kind of a name is Heartswallow?" she asked.

"It's Impish," Natterjack replied.

"What is 'Impish'?"

"I am."

"You are what?" She was beginning to get frustrated.

"Don't be obtuse, child; I am Impish, as anyone can plainly see."

"Don't make fun of me. I can't *plainly see* anything in this place," the Toad snapped.

"You're a bit high-strung for a toad, aren't you?" It was more of a statement than a question.

"Listen, Mr. Heartswallow, if you were having the kind of day that I have been having, you'd be upset, too."

"I should have realized that you weren't yet accustomed to the darkness," he continued as if he hadn't heard her. "I guess it's a good thing you're not. Here, let me help."

She felt a hard poke in the middle of her forehead, and her rescuer said a word she had never heard before.

"Hey!" she croaked indignantly, but before she could say another word, she realized that something had changed. She could see. She couldn't see very well or very far, maybe a hop or two into the darkness, but at least she could see a little.

She turned in excitement to say, "I can see!" and froze. A creature unlike any she had ever seen stood next to her. He was at least two feet tall—many times taller than she— and was one-eyed with long twisted tangles of serpentine-like hair that ended in brightly colored beads and a knitted cap on his head. It was smiling at her.

"As I said." This time his voice held no formality. "Name's Natterjack. Pleased to meet you."

CHAPTER FOUR

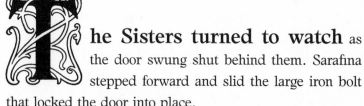he Sisters turned to watch as the door swung shut behind them. Sarafina stepped forward and slid the large iron bolt that locked the door into place.

"Grisswell!" Emilina called. "Seal the room. Bind it so that only I may enter."

"Annd youra Siss-ter?" The words seemed to slither from all around them.

"You have your instructions," Emilina said sharply. "You are invoked and you must abide!"

"Yes," the voice replied in such an inhuman growl that to the Sisters it sounded like "Yea esah."

Emilina turned and looked up at Sarafina, who was staring down at her with an ever-increasing frown.

"Sarafina," she said almost wearily, "you know that I

can't allow you to go into the Kitchen without me, especially now that the Toad is loose. Unless"—she paused—"you would like to take this with you to show you the way?" She held out the Book as if to offer it to her sister.

Looking down, Sarafina winced and stepped back, her eyes widening.

"Em-Emilina," she stuttered. "The Book...your blood is..."

Emilina glanced down and saw a single bright red spot on the upper right corner of the Book. If anyone had been closely examining Emilina's expression at that moment they might have noticed a tremor pass through her iron facade. Then again, it happened so quickly they might not. When Sarafina looked into her sister's face, Emilina was as impassive as stone.

"That's quite enough, Sarafina. Calm down. You are obviously still shaken by your failure in the Kitchen." Sarafina scowled. "Go to your room and collect yourself. Meet me in the study in one hour. I must clean myself and see to my injury."

"I can help bandage your..."

"You've 'helped' me quite enough for the time being," Emilina interrupted. "Now go!"

Sarafina turned and lumbered down the stone hallway. Emilina watched her until she rounded the corner and stepped out of sight.

Emilina took three steps in the opposite direction, paused, and said to the empty hallway, "Grisswell...do it now." She then continued along the shadowed corridor. As she passed out of the candlelight into the darkness, the click of her heels on the stone floor became faster and faster until they faded away into silence.

The hall was empty. In the stillness, a small cloud of dust lifted and began whirling on the floor. It churned and grew, reaching up toward the ceiling. The shadows in the dark spaces of the hall elongated and bled toward it. It grew into a spiraling dust storm, the shadows forming into veins of darkness weaving into its axis, gathering weight and solidity as it progressed. A figure began to emerge, and as it did so the dust devil dissipated and fell back to the floor.

Grisswell had a broad smile, full of sharp and broken teeth, across his misshapen face. He had three searing eyes that sat one atop the other on his long sloping forehead. His head and shoulders bore a mantle of twisted, black horns and he kept his wings folded tightly against his back.

The huge demon lifted his gnarled, taloned hand and gestured at the Kitchen door. Nothing happened.

He jerked his head to the side like a bird and stared at the door quizzically. "What is thissss? Why does the door deny my command?"

Grisswell stared at it, motionless for nearly ten minutes, before his eyes suddenly widened and he began to laugh. It was a horrible, grating sound like rusted metal grinding against rough stone. "It doesn't want to be ssealedah.

"There are other waysss, door." The demon spread his

long, heavily sinewed arms wide, took an enormous breath, and then brought his clawed hands together in an intricate gesture as he exhaled forcefully.

His steaming breath visibly impacted the Kitchen door, which began to ripple like water. The wood of the door began to crawl, as if it were ivy creeping over a castle wall. It continued to grow and writhe until not even the immense iron bolt could be seen through the dense tangle of living wood, branches, and vines. As an afterthought the

demon snapped his fingers, and large, black-tipped thorns sprouted across its entire surface.

"Anything worth doing," he chuckled to himself, "is worth overdoing."

As he sat cross-legged on the floor, his smile once again cracked across his face. With the serrated claw of his gnarled, bony finger he began to scratch images of Emilina and Sarafina on the dusty floor.

CHAPTER FIVE

he Toad looked around at her surroundings in stunned silence.

"What's your name?"

She glanced up at him with a look that was part confusion, part awe. Though her vision didn't stretch very far, the bits that she could see were strange. When Jack had said they were in a kitchen, she hadn't imagined this. She could make out the edges of cabinets, tables, and other furnishings, which would have been normal enough in an ordinary cottage or keep. But these things were not right. They felt...alive. The claw-footed table to her left was made of wood but looked as though it had just paused between steps, one leg slightly bent and raised off the floor. No one made tables like that, did they? She looked at Jack again to ask but as soon as she did a dash of movement made her look back. The table was gone. She looked around to the cabinet that they were standing beside and took a startled hop back. It had crooked fingers for handles. They weren't moving but as she looked at them she had the feeling that when she turned away they might writhe like knuckled worms. The thought made her shiver.

"What...is...your...name?" Natterjack repeated the question, this time very slowly and deliberately.

Since waking and finding herself held upside down over a seething cauldron, things had happened so fast that she hadn't had any time to reflect on her situation. Now, Natterjack had asked her a very simple question and when she tried to answer him she made a startling discovery: "I don't know."

"What do you mean?" said Natterjack, his brow furrowing over his large green eye.

"I mean I don't know what my name is," she said.

"Do you have a name? I've met other toads and they've all had names." He bent to look into her eyes. "Usually something like Stulmuck or Grumph. I met a turtle once that called himself Spontaneous Tump."

"I don't know," she said again as she nervously took a step back from him, her eyes widening in realization. "I can't remember anything!"

"Wait, don't get upset. What do you mean?...Can you remember anything before you fell into the nest? You landed pretty hard." Natterjack spoke to her in a low voice, trying to calm her.

"No!" She was still nearly shouting. "I remember falling. I remember everything after I woke up over the big pot, but nothing before that!"

"I said, keep your voice down. Now, wait. I'm confused. What pot? What do you mean?" Natterjack asked.

"I...don't...remember...anything! That's what I mean!"

Natterjack kneeled and looked her straight in the eyes. "Listen to me very carefully, Toad. If you don't stop croaking at the top of your lungs I am going to leave you here and be on my way."

"No, don't!" she said, immediately lowering her voice and stepping forward. "Please don't."

"That's better," he said. "I don't want to leave you, but you have to understand that there are things in this room that are extraordinarily dangerous. As dark as it is here, some of those things are attracted to sound. If you keep shrieking like that, then something will find us and there are creatures roaming this place that I'd rather not have to deal with. If you want my help, then you will listen to me. Do you understand that?"

"Okay, I understand," she said softly. "Please don't leave me." She sagged into a squat on the floor.

Natterjack sat in front of her. "You have to follow the rules of survival."

"I don't know those, either," she said, her gaze dropping.

"Well, you know the first one..." He paused for her to finish.

"No yelling," she said. "Or too much noise."

"Right." He smiled at her, and though she was still afraid and confused, his sincerity and concern gave her a boost. "I'll teach you the others but maybe you should tell me what you remember first. Start at the beginning."

She told him her tale, though it was short, from the cauldron to the nest. "What happened back there? Who were you talking to just before you pulled me out?"

"At the pinfetcher nest? The female; she came back as I was talking to you. When I heard you fall into her nest, I grabbed one of her pins before sneaking up to it. It's one of those self-defense skills you'll learn here. If the 'fetcher comes back, then all you have to do is lob the pin as far as you can and it scurries off to find it. She never would have left, though, if she'd known you were in there. Come here, take a look."

Natterjack got to his feet, stepped over to a nearby table, and glanced around it. He turned to the Toad, put one finger to his lips, made the "shhh" gesture, and then motioned for her to look at what he had seen. She crept over and took a peek.

Not a few leaps from them, she could see the nest. She was startled to realize how close they were to it. Hadn't they walked farther than this when she escaped its insides? It certainly felt like it. She looked up at Natterjack and he pointed to the base of the nest. She looked back just in time to see a creature, not much bigger than herself, step out from behind it.

The pinfetcher was like a fish, darting back and forth on two sinewy legs that looked more like arms. It had a silver sliver of metal in its protruding beaklike mouth and it appeared to be tidying up. It found a spot for its pin and carefully placed it. It stepped back, surveyed its handiwork, and emitted a soft, short birdlike trill. The Toad noticed that there were other sharp and jagged items protruding from the nest; bits of broken glass, thorns from unknown plants, and pieces of rusty wires were laced throughout.

They stepped away from the corner.

"It doesn't look very mean," she said.

"Normally they aren't aggressive at all," he replied. "You just have to leave their nest alone. They're very shy and they build their homes to keep the other creatures at bay."

"I think it works. But how come you didn't get scratched by the pins?"

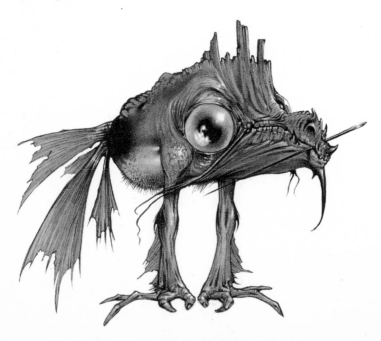

Natterjack lowered his hands and slowly wiggled his fingers. "It would take a lot more than those little spikes and barbs to do any damage to these." He tapped his left forearm with the knuckle of his right index finger. It made a metallic *crunk* sound.

"Is that an imp thing?" she asked.

"An imp thing? Ha! That's funny. No, it's not an 'imp' thing. It's a 'curse' thing," he replied. "The Witches wanted to punish me, so they gave me iron hands."

"Oh my god. That's terrible. Why?" she said, looking up at him.

"I was an artist, a painter of great renown in my clan. I lived to create. Those two sneaks wanted my talents. They lured me into the Kitchen and then tried to magically steal my ability to paint. When they couldn't ... you should have seen how angry Emilina was."

"Who is Emilina?" the Toad asked.

"The one that looks like a broom turned upside down."

"How come they couldn't steal your talent?"

"How can you steal how someone thinks? Art is in the mind, not in the hands," he replied. "How can you steal my ability to see beauty? Imps are beings of magic, and while they can steal my magic, what I could do was more than that ... it was a natural gift. They could not separate me from myself; they couldn't steal who I am."

"But those hands. You can't possibly be an artist with those." She paused. "Are you sad?"

"I am sad that I can't paint, but I'm still an artist."

"How can you be an artist if you can't do it anymore?"

Natterjack shrugged. "I'm an artist because I'm still me. I still see beauty wherever it is." He touched a piece of ornate carving that trimmed a nearby chair. "These hands aren't much good for holding a brush anymore but they are good for other things." He paused and gave her a rather mischievous smile. "And I'm learning how to sculpt stone."

She paused for a moment as another question occurred to her. "I couldn't understand the Witches when they spoke but I can understand you. Why?"

"We can understand each other because I am an imp. I speak Toad. I speak almost all common animal tongues, even though most don't have much to say. All imps can do it. It's in our nature."

"I wish I knew what they wanted from me. I wish I could remember who I am," she said, looking into the darkness.

"Well, you're outta luck there. I'm an imp, not a djinn. I can't grant you any wishes. Wishes are overrated anyway. It's sort of a cheat to wish for something, then wait for it to happen. Now if you had said, 'I want to find out what they want from me. I want to find out what's going on. I want to find out who I am,' well, then we could do something."

"What? What could we do?" She turned to him.

"We could go see the Widows of the Clock. They can help you get some answers if they're in the mood. They aren't that easy to find but we might get lucky."

"How will they know? It doesn't matter. Can we try?

28

Will you help me?" The Toad had to use all of her restraint to keep from squealing.

"Yes...we can. It's the best way to find out what's going on and I think we should set about it right away. I am beginning to think we don't have any time to lose."

"Why? What's wrong?" she asked, growing concerned.

"Something weird is happening that I can't quite explain."

"Weirder than everything already is?" she said, laughing a little, but glancing around for danger, then back at Natterjack.

"I don't quite know what this means but..." He paused. "And I didn't notice it when it started because it was a subtle change and, like I said, I speak a lot of tongues."

"Would you PLEASE tell me what you are talking about?" she said, restraining herself only barely enough to lower her voice.

"You're not speaking Toad anymore." He was still looking at her with his bright green eye. "You're speaking Impish."

CHAPTER SIX

Alone in her room, Sarafina sat on the edge of her huge four-poster bed. Pushed back so that its tall headboard rested against the far wall, it totally obscured the only window in the room. Made of thick, rough-hewn timbers, the bed was covered in linens and throws that were yellowed with age. There were patches and mismatched pieces that were sewn together with simple black thread.

The armchairs—there were two but no one except Sarafina had ever sat in either of them—were constructed with heavy legs and armrests and positioned around a small, sturdily built table in a corner. Covered in soft materials that looked worn and threadbare, they were patched and sewn in the same curious manner as the bed linens—as if they had been infinitely patched for a great many years.

A tarnished brass oil lamp cast flickering yellow light on the drooping tapestries that clung to the stone walls.

Sarafina, huge and brooding as she was, had an affinity for delicate, finely crafted things. The tragedy of this was that items of refinement could not bear her heavy-handed attention for very long. As careful as she tried to be, she was always mending her belongings.

Grunting, she descended onto one knee. With some difficulty she leaned forward, peering into the cavernous darkness under her bed, searching. "Ahhh," she said as she slid the dollhouse into view.

It was grotesque and it bore little resemblance to an actual dollhouse. A mishmash of pinned, nailed, twined, twisted, and wired pieces of wooden lath and worn materials were bound together in a mockery of a child's plaything.

The most disturbing aspect of the dollhouse, however, was its inhabitants. Engaged in a solitary silent tea party, the newest addition to her collection was a small, cracked, but finely detailed porcelain doll resting on a dainty wood chair. One of the chair's legs had been lost and Sarafina had used a long silver pin in its place. The doll's small hands lay on its lap cradling a tiny, shattered teacup. In another corner the battered form of a carved dog had porcelain human feet wedged onto the sharpened stumps of its own broken legs. Sprawled on the floor of the dollhouse there lay another figure made of loosely sewn canvas, but time and the continued abuse of Sarafina's attentions had rendered it stringy and clotted. It had no hands or feet. Its head was made of clay and upon it was sculpted the face of a wailing infant that was eerily lifelike. There were other figurines and effigies but few of them maintained a shape that anyone but Sarafina could appreciate.

They were strange-looking and sad but they weren't enchanted. Sarafina could have animated the little figures but she hadn't for two reasons: First, she wanted to keep them hidden, and magic might have alerted her sister to them and second, well...they were dolls and as patchwork as they were, she enjoyed their simplicity. Sarafina was a consummate spell worker but she did tire of it on occasion, unlike Emilina, who seemed to live for nothing else.

The most unusual member of this collection of oddities wasn't a doll of any sort. In the back right corner lay an intricately woven bowl of small branches, twigs, and strings—a nest. It was actually quite beautiful compared to the rest of the hodgepodge contents of the little structure. Sarafina thought it was the most perfect thing she had ever found.

Sarafina continuously mumbled to herself as she examined her prized possessions. She picked up each little figure in turn but when she began to reach for the nest she paused. It was the only whole and unbroken artifact in the entire assemblage. She left it untouched.

If she had picked up the nest she might have noticed the small silver pin that had become entangled in its wall—but considering how distracted and upset she was, she might not have.

Playing with her collection was a ritual that Sarafina always indulged in whenever she was emotional. And with a sister like Emilina she found herself peering into the maw of her ramshackle dollhouse *quite* often. Usually it had a calming effect upon her, but today the little figures, and especially the nest, only reminded her of the crib and how it had ruined everything so thoroughly.

"It wasn't me," she stated, as she slid the dollhouse back under the massive bed. "And she won't let it alone. She'll be at me about it even after it's fixed and we've found the Toad."

She hoisted herself off the floor using the solid post of her bed for support and walked over to the double doors of her closet. She opened the doors, reached in, and unlatched the lid of a large oak coffer. Though she could easily lift the entire chest with one hand, she merely tapped the lid with the knuckle of her index finger and it slowly creaked open by itself. She pulled out a hand-size leather pouch and a twined bundle of yellow candles. As she turned and placed the items on the bed, the chest closed and fastened itself silently behind her.

She paused, rubbing her furrowed brow with the palm of her left hand, and said, "And if she's not worried about the Book gettin' a drink of her insides, why should I?"

Emilina's room was plain and unadorned, barely a room at all. It contained only three pieces of furniture: a simple upright wooden chair, a nightstand standing next to the bed, and the bed itself. There were no pictures or hangings on the walls, no curtains on the window, and, except for the carvings on the door, no decorative elements at all. She did not live here. She merely slept here. Emilina lived in the Kitchen.

Right now, she was worried. There were certain rules that governed her craft, especially when it came to the use of the Book. She had discovered these guidelines over the years with the Kitchen and the Book. One rule and perhaps the most crucial was: Never, never leave the Book unattended in the Kitchen. It had happened only once and, well...she didn't let herself think about that. Another rule that she had discovered early on was that the Book must be...fed. Late one night she had left a caged rat on her nightstand next to the Book. In the early morning hours, sometime before dawn, she had woken to a solitary squeal. She had lit a candle and the Book was lying where she had left it, except that it was open and the rat and its cage had vanished. For the next few days the Book became easier to use, easier to read, at least for her.

Sarafina had never been able to discern a single page of the Book. It didn't surprise Emilina. It took forceful,

directed willpower and concentration to bring its pages into focus, and to be blunt, her sister was only focused when she was angry. It was strange that the Book did not respond to anger. It seemed to prefer cold, calculating thought.

Emilina set the Book on her nightstand while she cleaned herself and put her injured nose to rights. When she returned, the Book lay open. She picked it up but the pages it showed were blank. It was when she closed the Book that she noticed it. The spot of blood on the cover was gone.

She inhaled through her teeth and dropped the Book on her bed.

Now she sat in her chair as rigid as the stone wall behind her, staring intensely at the Book as it lay in the center of her bed. It chased the light from the room and the faded yellow of her unpatterned bed linens turned grey in a circle surrounding it.

"What does it mean?" she whispered. "Does it mean anything?" Across the room the Book slowly opened itself and lay still, waiting for her to read its answer.

CHAPTER SEVEN

Sarafina sat at the large oak table centered in the study, books strewn in front of her. All four walls of the study were lined with books, breaking only where the one door led into the room, rows and rows of archaic tomes and large leather-bound volumes of various shapes and sizes.

The room itself was illuminated by five levitating glass spheres that looked as though they were filled with fireflies and hovered gently, swaying as if alive.

"Deimus," Sarafina said, "look here." She tapped the open page of a particularly old and moldy volume. A little glowing ball slowly drifted over and brightened slightly to better illuminate the text as Sarafina examined it. Then suddenly, the little orb bolted to the far corner of the room and cowered with the other four spheres.

Sarafina was startled to see Emilina standing on the

other side of the table, cradling the Book in one arm, like an infant.

"What are you doing, Sister?" Emilina asked as she glanced down at the pile of codices and ancient bindings.

"You were late"—Sarafina paused, anticipating a retort from her sister, but surprisingly, none came—"...and I thought to look in some of these for an idea about how to find the Toad. The Kitchen won't make it easy."

"The Kitchen isn't what caused this mess," Emilina said as she glared at her sister, "but you are quite right, the little beast will be wretched difficult to find. The Kitchen does like to hide things and there is the matter of time, as well. If we don't complete the ritual, and soon, there will be...repercussions."

"What do you mean?" asked Sarafina. "What's going to happen?"

"We don't have time to discuss it now, Sarafina, and as you have already pointed out, we're late."

"Fine," Sarafina said, exasperated, and reached for a book. "Let me show you what I've found."

"Nothing in these feeble guides will aid us," Emilina said dismissively.

"Then why did you want to meet in the study?"

"Because," Emilina answered, "we need those." She

pointed at the little spheres of light trembling in the corner.

"How can the deimus help? Even if they could *find* the Toad, they couldn't lift her."

"Let me show you," Emilina said. She held up her left hand and one of the spheres shot across the room and into her palm with a loud smack.

She laid the Book on the table in front of her, held the radiating orb over the black cover, and slowly began to lower it. The little light struggled in Emilina's hand, but she held it steady. It began to emit a high-pitched warbling whistle.

"What is it doing?" Sarafina asked.

"It's screaming," Emilina said flatly.

The very moment the little glass sphere touched the cover of the Book it fell silent and motionless. Emilina took her hand away and the bauble slowly sank into the liquid black of the cover and disappeared.

Turning to look behind her, Emilina said, "Crine, come here." And from the shadows in the hall, through the open doorway, sharp, hooked talons clicked against the stone floor. Like Sarafina's tiny crib, it was a creature of white bone and black beak, with one shining black eye, but it was perhaps ten times as large. The crine was graceful, fluid, and reptilian. It leaped lithely to the tabletop, and Emilina pointed at the Book and said, "In."

The crine leaned forward with its beak to touch the Book's cover, but as it did so the ebony beak seemed to merge with the blackness of the binding and the skeletal creature slid into the darkness like the deimus.

Emilina smiled at her sister. "It won't take long. You'll see."

Almost immediately, the Book regurgitated the crine. The limp body spewed forth from the cover with a wet, gurgling sound and flopped onto the table covered in a milky, yellow slime.

It stirred. Ever so slowly, like a newborn colt, it made its way upright on unsteady legs. It shook its head from side to side, like a wet dog, slinging stringy slime in an arc across the

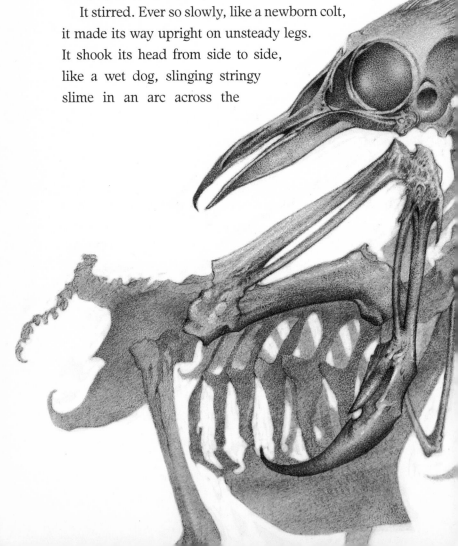

table and the floor. Gradually it began to regain its lizard-like composure.

Sarafina, eyes open wide in amazement, exclaimed, "It's changed!"

And she was right.

The crine had grown larger. Its talons were longer and sharper, the skull tapered back into thin, spiraling horns, and where its single black eye had been, the deimus radiated a cool bluish light. Behind the lattice of the rib cage was a small and finely wrought silver cage that was just the right size for a toad. The creature scanned from left to right as if it were hungry and searching for food.

As Emilina and Sarafina watched the foul thing walk up and down the table another crine entered the room, and then a third, a fourth, and a fifth.

Each one was likewise transformed in its turn and afterward, as they paced the room looking for prey, their new eyes cast beams of light on the rows of books and the cold stone floor.

Emilina glanced around, looking at her contingent of skeletal servants. She smiled a thin, flat smile that did not reach her eyes and said, "Are they not sweet, Sarafina? So obedient...and so hungry."

Sarafina did not answer.

 **should have done this before,"** Natterjack said as he sat down in front of the Toad.

"What are you going to do?"

"Well," he began, "I have a limited ability to see magical traces. I should have read you the moment you mentioned that the Witches were interested in you."

"What could they want from me? I mean, I'm just a toad. I can't do anything."

"Can't do anything? You just learned how to speak Impish in two minutes without ever having heard it. That's doing something." He stared at her, his one eye unblinking and bright.

She didn't like being scrutinized. Squirming, she asked,

"Shouldn't we be going? You said we had to hurry. Do we have time for this?"

Jack ignored her. "Do you want to know what I don't get?" He paused. "Except for the minor night-sight glimmer that I put on you, you show no signs of magic cast upon you. I suppose it could be a natural talent. But since I have never met another toad that could speak Impish, I am going to go right ahead and assume that something is going on. And possibly ongoing."

"I really don't have any idea what you're saying. Can we be 'ongoing' now?" Her impatience was edging up on her.

"Yes, yes. It's time to get moving. We've been in one spot too long as it is." He stood and looked around. "Which way to start, though...hmmm. A good start is halfway home, as they say."

"Could you please stop talking in riddles?"

"Don't worry about it. It just means to think about where you want to go before you run off in the wrong direction. It also means to be prepared but since we have no idea what's going on, we're about as prepared as we can be right now."

"So how do we make a good start? I mean if we don't know which way to go."

"Well, the Kitchen is a difficult place to navigate. It likes to keep its pantry to itself, so to speak. Have you noticed by now that the room changes? It kind of reorganizes itself, constantly."

"I *knew* that we had walked farther from that nest than it seemed when we saw it again!"

"Yup. This place is different from moment to moment. Sometimes a little, sometimes a lot," he said, "but, like I said before, I know how to get by. The first thing we have to do is set our eyes on Ol' Guthrie."

"Who is Ol' Guthrie? Is he safe?" the Toad asked.

"Not exactly. I mean he's safe enough, but we're not really going to meet him." Natterjack smiled and shook his head in amusement. "Ol' Guthrie occupies the only spot in the whole Kitchen that doesn't seem to move. It's a real mystery, but sometimes it can help to start at his place."

"Okay, so how do we find him?"

"We close our eyes and listen." And as he said it, he did it.

The Toad did the same, then cocked one eye open and asked, "What are we listening for?"

"Can you hear the sounds of the Kitchen?" he asked as he slowly turned his head from side to side.

"I...can hear something," she whispered. "It sounds like...like..."

"It sounds like tables and chairs and crates and other things gently shuffling across the floor. Listen for a direction in which you hear no sounds at all. It's easier with your eyes closed."

With her eyes shut tightly she slowly turned her head from side to side, as she had seen the imp do. "I think I have it!" she said as she paused and opened her eyes again.

"I think you do, too." She and Natterjack were both looking in the same direction.

"This is the way...the good start?" she asked.

"It's as good as it's likely to get." He nodded toward the silence. "Time to get going. Stay close, okay? I'd hate to lose you."

"Don't worry," she said. "I'd hate to be lost."

"Either way, I'd be able to find you eventually. With that night-sight spell I put on you, you're trackable. So don't get lost, but don't panic if you do, either. We're incredibly lucky that the Witches hadn't already cast a spell on you or they would be able to find you instantly."

Natterjack began to walk, and, true to her word, with small tentative hops, the Toad stayed as close to him as she could. They hadn't gone very far when she asked him, "How big is this room anyway?"

"Kitchen," he corrected her.

"Okay, how big is the Kitchen?"

"You wouldn't believe me if I told you." He put his finger to his lips for the third time.

"It can't be that big," she whispered.

"That all depends on your point of view," he said in a low voice.

She was getting incredibly sick of Natterjack's inability to answer a question directly.

Natterjack looked down at her and could see that she was frustrated by his answer. "I promise to tell you more but we need to be quiet right now. Okay?"

She still looked uneasy but nodded in agreement.

They walked (and hopped) in a zigzag path around tables, crates, and cupboards. The Toad quickly learned not to look behind them because as they passed an area it would change, but only when it wasn't being watched. It was disconcerting to look behind herself and not see the place that she had just come from, so she kept her eyes forward. That didn't help much either because she soon discovered that there were many more creatures here than she would have believed. Nearly every step they took brought the sound of things scurrying. They turned a particular corner and stumbled upon a large insectlike creature. It had no eyes, two mouths, and a beetle-like shell. It turned toward them and smiled with human teeth, the body of a rat hanging out of one of its mouths.

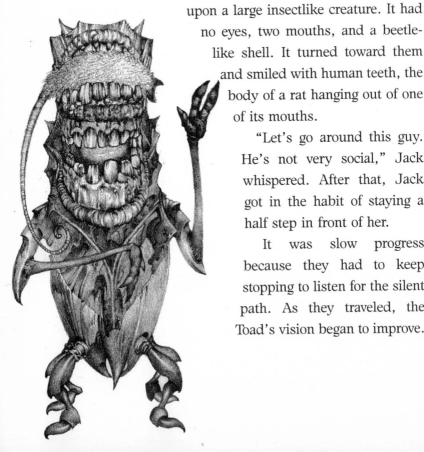

"Let's go around this guy. He's not very social," Jack whispered. After that, Jack got in the habit of staying a half step in front of her.

It was slow progress because they had to keep stopping to listen for the silent path. As they traveled, the Toad's vision began to improve.

She could see a little farther than before, fine details were more apparent, and every now and then colors began to seep back through the gloomy shadow. She could even see the wood grain on the table legs as they passed. She turned to whisper her surprise to Natterjack and realized that he had stopped walking.

"What's wrong?" she said, seeing that he was staring down into the darkness to their left. He did not look happy.

She followed his line of sight and inhaled sharply when she saw what had caught his eye. Standing between two table legs was the little skeletal bird. It stepped forward and clicked its beak. She scurried closer to Natterjack and whispered, "That's it! That's the thing that attacked the big witch and then me."

Natterjack's voice was low and cautious. "That's just a crib," he said. "I can handle a crib." He paused, then looked up over the bony little thing. "It's his big brother that might be a problem."

"What?" she said as her gaze followed his.

The little crib made a nervous hop forward and as it did the table legs it stood between began to move. Surprised, the Toad took a harder look at them in the darkness. They were legs, but of course they weren't table legs as the Toad had thought. They were bone white, which was appropriate, since they were actually bones, and they ended in a pair of very wicked-looking talons. The Toad looked up at the creature. It did look a little like the crib but Natterjack wasn't joking when he called it the crib's big brother. However, something else really caught her eye about the thing.

A cage. It's got a cage for guts, and it wants to swallow me, the Toad realized.

The thing stepped forward and its single eye began to glow. The bluish beam fell first on Natterjack's face, then quickly shifted to the Toad. It parted its enormous black beak and made a shrieking, bleating sound, like a cross between a vulture and a goat. Answering shrieks sounded in the distance.

Natterjack stepped between the creature and the Toad. The beast lowered its head and hissed at him. "This isn't just a crine! Crines don't look like this. They don't act like this."

Natterjack made his hands into fists and raised them. Then, as the creature sprang at him, the Toad heard him say one more thing. "Crap."

CHAPTER NINE

He's *winning,* the Toad thought as she watched the imp and the crine lunge at and dodge each other. Natterjack's iron hands didn't slow him down at all. In fact, he used their added weight to his advantage. More than once when the crine thrust forward Jack blocked the razor-sharp end of the beak with one arm and slammed a big metal fist into the creature's side as it slid past him. He managed to fight with grace, and his defenses appeared to be taking a toll on the crine as its attacks became less aggressive and more wary.

The crine and Natterjack circled each other, both stilling their attacks for a moment. Finally, in apparent exasperation, the crine backed up a pace and just stood there.

It kept its illuminating eye fixed on Natterjack's face, contemplating its next move.

"Hey, Toad, you okay?" he asked without turning to look at her.

Her heart was nearly thumping out of her chest but she said, "Yeah, I'm okay."

"I'm warning you ahead of time: I'm going to kill this thing. Don't freak out—it's not really alive. It hasn't been for a very long time."

"Okay," she said in a tremulous voice. She was scared, but she didn't really have any sympathy for the brutal creature.

Natterjack lunged. He caught the crine by surprise, going on the offensive so suddenly that it couldn't react as the imp's iron fist swung down in a destructive arc across the bridge of its beak, splintering the bony material and stunning it for a brief second. It was more than enough time for Natterjack to bring his other fist into action.

The second strike smashed directly into the crine's glowing eye. It exploded with a flash and sent out little sparks of light that wriggled around like tadpoles until they faded into darkness.

Natterjack stood frowning down at the shattered crine at his feet. "Well, it may not look like a regular crine but destroy the eye and it dies like one."

"Is it really dead?" the Toad asked.

Natterjack prodded the bones with his boot. "Bustin' the eye is the only nonmagical way of destroying a crine.

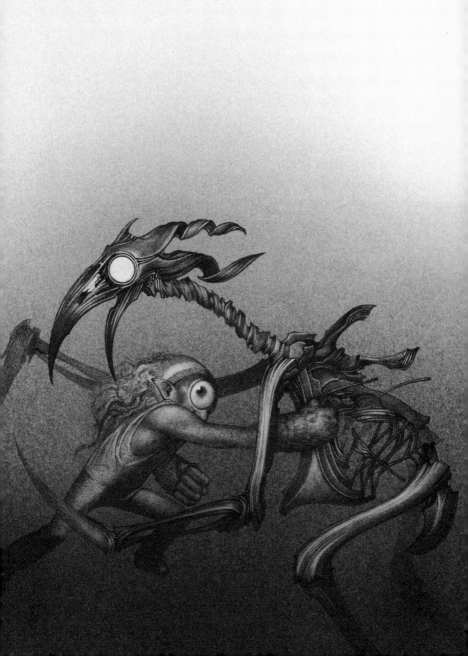

If I didn't have these..." He flexed his metal hands. "But yeah, it's as dead as it should be. This thing is weird, though. It definitely looks like a crine, but it's been altered. Do you see that thing in its ribs?"

She nodded. "A cage. It's for me, isn't it?"

"That's a safe bet," he said as he glanced at the fallen form. "They don't usually have that. Or glowing spotlight eyes, for that matter."

Just then a little spark of light squirmed past her foot toward the crine. "Hey!" she cried. "Look!"

Natterjack watched the little points of light crawl over the skeletal bird and make their way up to the empty eye socket. The crine's foot spasmed and its claw clicked against the floor. "Let's get outta here before..." Suddenly, four beams of light found him in the darkness.

They were surrounded. There were five exits between cabinets, sideboards, and tables. Altered crines stood in four of them, and the fifth crine was only moments from reanimating. Natterjack scooped up the Toad and sprinted toward the fallen creature. It snapped at him with its broken beak as he leaped over it. But the Toad could already hear the sounds of the other crines pursuing them as the imp ran full-out, zigzagging his way around tables, chests, and the other debris of the Kitchen.

The crines definitely had the advantage of height and the agility of birds. Skittering and flitting across the tops of the obstacles that Natterjack had to navigate around, the creatures were gaining on their prey. As the skeletal birds closed in on Natterjack and the Toad, they began to bleat and shriek to each other.

"I don't believe this. They're communicating with each other . . . organizing!" the imp gasped.

Though Natterjack and the Toad were small, the crines were too close for them to be able to hide anywhere. He continued on, in and out, around and under, but still they drew closer. Finally Natterjack rounded a corner and ran headlong into a sideboard that closed off his escape. He turned to face the creatures, putting the Toad down behind him as he did.

"I can keep them here. You're going to have to run," he ordered. "Now."

"No! I'll be lost!" she croaked.

"I'll find you. Remember? The night sight. I'll find you again."

"Promise?"

"I promise. I will find you. Now go!" She flattened herself as low as her pliable, squatted body would go and crawled underneath the sideboard.

She saw the black, hooked claws of the crines and Natterjack's booted feet as she backed farther into the darkness. The sideboard rocked on its short legs as something slammed into it and she scurried out the other side. She heard another loud crash and Impish swearwords. She had to stay close. Maybe under the cabinet so that she could still see his feet, but when she turned and looked back . . . the cabinet was gone.

The room had changed. She couldn't see any movement and the sounds of fighting seemed very far away now. They were moving farther and farther away until she could hear nothing but the whispered shuffling of the Kitchen itself.

She was alone. The Toad did not like being alone. Her heart beat frantically in her chest as she began to panic. Something made a small scraping noise nearby and she leaped to her right, nearly screeching in fear. She looked over her shoulder and saw what appeared to be a common garden cricket scratching its way up a table leg. She stopped, her breath caught in her throat.

It examined her with human eyes.

Repulsed and horrified, she backed away from the insect. It stared at her for a moment longer, then continued on its way.

Unable to stop herself, she turned and fled. Running and hopping as fast as she could manage, she darted this way and that.

She ran and began to cry. The tears, filling her eyes and blurring her vision, ran down her cheeks. She had to stop when she couldn't see where she was going any longer. She still wanted to run but she dared not.

She wiped her eyes and in that brief clarity of vision she saw a cracked clay bowl lying on its side near a wrought-iron stand. She walked over to it, gripped it by its edge, and pulled it over herself. She crouched there under the bowl, looking out through the narrow crack in its lip, and the tears came again and her breath left her in sobs.

It seemed to her that she would cry herself away but then she remembered what Natterjack had told her about sound and the predators in the Kitchen. And she willfully slowed her breath. As she did, her heart slowed as well, and she discovered that she was exhausted. She didn't really feel safe under her crockery, but she did feel hidden and she finally started to relax.

CHAPTER TEN

The day was bright and crisp. A perfect blue sky lay open before her as she flew. The small kestral falcon spread her wings and rose higher on a warm updraft almost without effort.

I can't believe it, she thought, but she flew as if she were the spirit of flight, reveling in her newfound mastery of the air. She sensed the patterns of air currents that lay before and behind her and she instantly knew how to navigate them. She didn't know where she was going and she didn't care. As she rose ever higher into that flawless, sparkling blue morning, one thought seemed to lift her even further: *I am free.*

In the distance, a small fleck caught her sharp eyes. She could see mice playing on the forest floor from more than a mile away, but this wasn't a mouse and it was coming at her very fast. In fact it was about to collide with her in midair, and in its blurring speed she realized too late what it actually was.

The arrow struck her in the chest and the blow took her breath. Gasping, she began to fall, and the radiant blue of the world began to bleed away into darkness. She waited for the impact, eyes tightly shut, wondering if she would feel it. Would it be terrible? Would it hurt? Long moments passed. She opened her eyes and found that she was no longer falling. She was standing on the ground and to her astonishment she raised her wing...but it wasn't a wing any longer. She flexed her now human hand in front of her, examining it. She raised her other hand. A thin silver chain dangled from her closed fist. She slowly opened her hand and a small, intricately carved silver falcon rested on her palm.

"It's so beautiful," she said, but as she did a chilling gust of wind raced over her and the carving crumbled into fine powder and was swept away.

"No," she cried softly as a second frigid draft crept over her. Where it touched her, the skin darkened to a pebbled, mottled green.

The Toad awoke. She had been dreaming and she found that in her sleep she had raised her arm in front of her as she had in the dream. For a moment her bulbous, warted arm looked foreign to her, as if it belonged to someone else.

She stared at it for a few long moments, then shook herself out of her thoughts.

"What a strange dream. I wonder what it means, if it means anything at all," she said. "But there's no sense wasting time on something I can't explain. All I can do now is try to find the silent path . . ."

She closed her eyes to listen, and in a moment she had it. She thought to herself: *I may be alone but I know which direction to go . . . at least for now.*

Even so, it was . . . difficult. For the last two hours the Toad had slowly, carefully made her way along the silent path. It was the only direction she knew she could go in. As she walked and hopped, she gradually became aware of a gnawing emptiness in her belly. Her hunger had crept up on her slowly but now was becoming so strong that she was having trouble keeping her mind focused on the path.

"I'm starving," she said, wishing somehow that the magic of the Kitchen would provide for her. She hadn't seen many creatures, nor had she seen food. On the bright side, her night vision had been steadily improving as she traveled.

This is serious, she thought. *What if I really do starve to death? How long does that take? Five days?* Not that she could guess how much time passed in the dark of the Kitchen. *I haven't seen a single thing to eat.*

At that moment she noticed a flicker of movement off to her left. A grasshopper, about two feet away. As she watched, it leaped into the air...and landed right in front of her. For a scant second the grasshopper looked up at the Toad and then it was gone.

And when she felt something wriggling in her mouth, she realized that she had snapped up the grasshopper by instinct alone. She didn't know what to do. A part of her mind was recoiling at the thought of consuming the bug, but her hunger was telling her to eat the thing. She thought, *Okay...I can do this,* and she summoned her will, trying to swallow the squirming mass. It was no use. Whatever instinct  that had snagged the grasshopper could not overcome her revulsion when it came time to eat it. She spat the disheveled insect out in a saliva-covered heap on the floor. The poor thing wasted no time and within two bounds it had fled her field of vision.

Great, she thought as she began to walk again. *Not only do I have total amnesia, but I must be the only toad in the world that can't eat bugs. The other toads must get a real kick out of that. I'll bet that wherever home is, I'm a total laughingstock. Well, laugh it up. I'm starving.*

Maybe...maybe I'm a vegetarian! But her excitement

once again deflated when she realized that she hadn't seen any plants in the Kitchen. There had been a few withered brown stems and weathered leaves here and there but nothing more. With no light, how could plants grow? Of course, there wouldn't be any water to feed them anyway.

"Water," she whispered to herself.

Great, now I'm thirsty, she thought. *And I want to get the taste of grasshopper out of my mouth. Guess what... that's right,* she said to herself, "No water, either!"

In the darkness a piercing pair of ice blue eyes watched the Toad. These eyes could see better in the dark than most animals could see in the light and they had observed, with interest, the incident with the grasshopper. It smiled with a mouth full of tiny, needle-sharp teeth and continued to stalk the Toad, at a distance.

The Toad had walked for perhaps ten minutes when she realized she had been so consumed with her hunger and thirst that she had not been paying attention to the path. She stopped and closed her eyes, calming herself to hear the sounds of the Kitchen. But it wasn't the silent path that next caught her attention. It was a smell that came through over the musky, dank odors that lay so close to the floor. *What is that?* she thought. *It smells... what? Fresh? Pure? How could anything smell fresh or pure down here? Unless...* Suddenly hopeful, she ran toward it.

She moved so fast that she almost fell right into it.

The Toad was staring down at a circular depression in the floor. Judging from the portion she could see in the dark she guessed it must be five or six feet wide. Most important, most amazing, a few inches down from where the stone floor sloped from her feet...water.

She moved cautiously toward the lip of the indentation, looking all around her like a gazelle at a watering hole. There was a large clearing around the puddle—even the furniture was far away. It made the Toad nervous, but she was thirsty enough to risk it.

As she came closer she saw that the water was sparkling and rippling as if there were brisk wind, but there was no wind, none at all. She crept closer still and realized that the water also glowed slightly. The light was ever so faint and it made her pause only for a moment. Her thirst had doubled when she had first smelled the water, and now seeing it had made it even worse.

Before the Toad could lower her head to the water, she saw something standing at the edge of a wooden structure— a slender silhouette. It stepped forward out of the darkness. It looked like a tiny slender girl...except for the wings.

"A fairy," the Toad whispered. "Well, are you going to attack me? I'm not afraid of you."

The fairy just stood there, her small eyes sparkling like sapphire embers as she gazed at the Toad. She smiled at her, displaying silver needlelike teeth. The Toad said, mostly to herself, "Well that's just creepy."

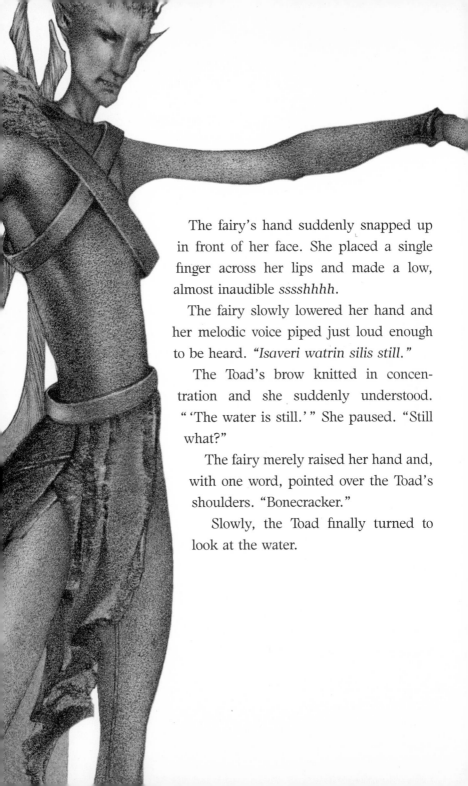

The fairy's hand suddenly snapped up in front of her face. She placed a single finger across her lips and made a low, almost inaudible *sssshhhh*.

The fairy slowly lowered her hand and her melodic voice piped just loud enough to be heard. *"Isaveri watrin silis still."*

The Toad's brow knitted in concentration and she suddenly understood. " 'The water is still.' " She paused. "Still what?"

The fairy merely raised her hand and, with one word, pointed over the Toad's shoulders. "Bonecracker."

Slowly, the Toad finally turned to look at the water.

CHAPTER ELEVEN

he Toad looked at the smooth surface of the motionless water. Whatever had been causing its rippling undulations before had stopped, but the soft, radiant light was getting noticeably brighter.

What now? she thought.

As the fairy stepped up to the edge of the well, the Toad didn't quite understand what she was seeing at first. It looked as if the fairy had detached her wings and was now holding them in her hands. On her back she wore a leather strap with two small loops and tiny silver buckles—odd. She'd never have guessed that a fairy would have to strap wings to her own back.

And then she understood. *Those aren't wings. They're swords!*

With a roar, the well suddenly burst into a tidal wave, knocking the Toad tail over teakettle, back against the random furniture that surrounded the well. The fairy stood perfectly motionless in what was now the only dry spot near the well. Not a drop of water had touched her.

The Toad looked up and saw the most horrendous thing she had ever seen. A serpentine form ran from beneath the water into the darkness above, covered in reptilian scales that shimmered with a dull, bluish glow, which was the only reason that she could still see its upper body, which stretched far above her, beyond the normal range of her night sight. At its midsection, it became segmented like an insect and at the intersection of each segment there was a long, thin pair of arms ending in a single wickedly sharp barb. At the top, there were two longer, stronger arms.

These did not have hands...they had meat cleavers. Two huge razor-sharp crablike pincers opened and closed, making a rapid clicking sound.

The Toad could not see its face. Long, thick, oily black tangles of hair hung down in front of where its face would have been. But she *could* see its eyes. Protruding bulbously on swaying finger-thick stalks from under the matted tangle of hair they looked like human eyes, but lidless and bloodshot...and they were glaring at her.

She quickly began looking for a way out, but all of the pathways and corners were blocked. The Kitchen had moved again and this time it didn't feel random. It felt like a betrayal. It felt like a trap. There was nowhere to go, nowhere to run. She looked back up at the horrendous thing that was twitching and trembling with rage. Their eyes met.

The Toad was horrified to discover that she couldn't take her eyes off the creature's stare.

She struggled against it but the Toad found she couldn't look away, no matter how hard she tried. She couldn't even blink.

The monster raised one of its meat cleaver hands high into the air, and slashed it down toward the Toad. Suddenly, the fairy lifted the tips of her swords and touched them together, creating a small, brilliant spark. It was enough. Distracted, the creature's claw miraculously changed course directly for the fairy. The claw connected solidly with the stone floor where the fairy stood, spraying fragments and stone splinters everywhere.

As soon as the monster broke eye contact with her, the Toad found that she could move again. She cringed, expecting to see the worst of what was left of the fairy. She knew she shouldn't care—the little beast probably just wanted to make her an entrée. But she didn't see the fairy there. To her astonishment, the fairy was standing to the left of where the creature's pincer was embedded in the stone, barely a hand's breadth from it, swords outstretched to both sides and her blue fire eyes open wide.

The Toad inhaled sharply in surprise as the fairy lightly jumped onto the back of the wicked-looking pincer. Moving slowly, the creature merely lifted the fairy to its eye level. They regarded each other for a moment. The fairy was obviously unaffected by the creature's paralytic gaze. The monster lifted its other claw and slowly scissored it open, and the fairy remained motionless. There was a blur of movement as the claw lurched forward and snapped shut.

The Toad flinched back in surprise as something landed in front of her with a wet thump, and then slowly, afraid of what she might see, she looked down to see a bloody mass. A huge severed eye looked dully back at her, its glow already fading. From above came a deafening roar of pain and fury.

Dizzy with shock, she suddenly saw that the fairy was standing next to her, though she had not heard or seen a thing. The fairy looked at the Toad with her unnerving, pointed little smile and said, "Now jumps the leaper, please." Startled, the Toad did. And it was not for nothing, because in that instant a claw struck the exact spot where she had been standing.

The fairy turned in a graceful pirouette with her swords a blur of motion to carve a divot of shell and meat from the bony pincer beside her. The creature bellowed again, whipping up the injured claw and arching its back, roaring and thrashing at the black air above them.

The monster twisted and turned, thrusting, snapping, and slapping at the fairy, all of its attention on the tiny flitting form. The fairy avoided the monster by a hair's width, ducking and dodging, leaping, twisting, and cutting. Sliced pieces of the bonecracker were falling all around. This seemed to have little or no effect on the flailing creature aside from infuriating it. Its attacks became faster and more vicious.

The fight was brutal and intense but soon it became painfully obvious that the fairy could not keep this pace up for much longer. She was beginning to tire. No longer able to attack with each turn and dive, she had to use all of her remaining speed and energy just to dodge pincers. She was on the defensive, and the monster was nowhere near letting up. Her graceful turns and leaps became more and more frantic and less graceful, and the last cleaving strike sent her rolling. She leaped immediately to her feet only to be struck solidly with a sweeping blow from the flat side of the bonecracker's other crablike claw. Swatted sideways, she flew face-first into a wooden cask at the edge of the well. She crumpled to the floor, her swords sliding from her hands and falling at her side.

The beast straightened itself at the ready, waiting for the fairy to stand again.

She did try. She pushed herself up on one arm and succeeded in rolling over onto her back. She continued to struggle as the monster opened and closed its claws in anticipation.

The Toad couldn't just stand there and watch. She had to do something. Sure, the fairy probably wanted to eat her, but the Toad couldn't stand by while a living creature was killed. The fairy had saved her, after all.

The Toad watched as the bonecracker cocked its head at the fairy and once more began to advance on her.

Maybe I can distract it, give her a moment to recover, she thought as she took a deep breath.

"*Croooaaakkk!*" To her credit, it was a very loud croak indeed, but nothing happened. The creature closed in on the sprawled, nearly unconscious fairy.

The Toad thought, *First I can't be quiet enough . . . and now I can't be loud enough.*

68

She tried again.

"Crooooooaaakkkkk!!" It was perhaps one of the loudest croaks that a toad had ever issued but still the creature began to raise its hideous claw.

But something strange was beginning to happen to the Toad. As she inhaled, taking an absolutely huge gulp of air, the mottled green and grey of her pebbled skin began to shimmer and change colors. First it morphed to olive, then aqua, then violet, then it started all over again.

To the Toad, the breath seemed to come from somewhere deeper inside than her lungs. Further down than even her broad, webbed feet. She felt as though she drew it from everywhere at once. It was not a croak or a yell. It felt like a thunderclap building inside her and when it burst forth from her open mouth it poured out like a hurricane wind.

It was actually visible for a moment. The sound was a shifting mass of color that slammed into the bonecracker like a solid wall of iron. It blasted the monster back and shattered it into pieces. The fairy collapsed. In the following moments, there were only the sounds of breaking glass and rustlings and scurryings as all sorts of hidden creatures fled the area.

As the resounding echo faded, the Toad slumped, too weak to remain standing. Her last thought before losing consciousness was, *Oh, that was loud,* and then darkness closed the door to her thoughts.

CHAPTER TWELVE

The Toad woke up and looked around. She was becoming used to waking up and not recognizing her surroundings. The one thing that had remained consistent was that the Kitchen was always changing, always different from moment to moment.

I'm still hungry and still thirsty, she thought.

Curiously, the well was gone—or at least she was gone from the well—but her vision had continued to improve.

I want to keep going. I want to find the path again. Of course, the fairy wasn't in eyesight. The Toad wasn't sure whether she should be nervous about this or not. The fairy had tried to save her, but perhaps it was because she didn't want the monster to steal her dinner.

She squatted for a moment to explore her improved

vision. Now there were half a dozen open spaces that she could use to escape this area, assuming that this was indeed where the well had been.

"Thanks for nothing," she whispered to the Kitchen. "Where were you when I needed those?"

She could see across the span of at least a dozen hops now. It seemed like a small victory until she realized that there was more space to be aware of, more hiding places to keep track of. There was movement as well. The occasional glimpse of some fleeting shape, the half-seen sparkle of a pair or multiple pairs of beady little eyes. It was as if suddenly the Kitchen, which had already seemed to harbor many strange creatures and oddities, became a city. But it felt untamed, like a forest.

She would have expected to be totally tense and exhausted, or at least sore from the previous commotion, but she felt incredible. She actually felt better than she had since she first woke up in the Kitchen. She was still hungry and thirsty but she wasn't as urgent about it. Almost getting split in two by the bonecracker had put things into perspective.

As she sat, her frog eyes caught a movement to her left. She snapped her head in that direction and saw the creature that had caused it: a strange, glowing slug. It was smaller than herself but she knew that didn't mean anything. Smaller could be just as deadly as larger if you weren't careful. The fairy was smaller than she but certainly formidable.

The shimmering little slug worked itself across the floor in a relatively straight line. It pulled itself along with a set of fingerlike appendages that protruded from its front end. The fingers' ends emitted a greenish glow, not unlike a firefly, but constant and steady rather than winking on and off. It extruded a thick glowing slime behind it.

It seemed oblivious to the Toad. As she watched, a moth fluttered down from somewhere, obviously attracted to the dimly luminous trail. It fluttered and flitted, and inadvertently its wing tip brushed the slug trail...and stuck. The little insect struggled for a moment but only became more immobile as other parts of its body came into contact with the slime.

A small pulse of light ran up the slime and when it reached the slug, the creature stopped, turned around, and slowly began to make its way back down the trail that it had just created. Where it crawled over the slime trail, it cleaned the floor. It seemed to be scooping up the slime into a hidden mouth on its underside. In a few moments it reached the moth and began to crawl over it. The moth panicked, wriggling futilely before disappearing beneath

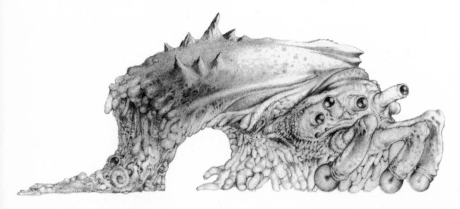

the slug. As the creature continued, there was nothing left but clean stone floor.

The Toad watched in fascination, and yes, a little revulsion, as the creature continued on and disappeared around a corner.

"Glue pooper," said a voice from behind her.

The Toad spun and found herself staring into a single enormous green eye.

CHAPTER THIRTEEN

ATTERJACK!!!"

"Did you know that you're being followed by a stickleback?" Natterjack asked.

The Toad flung herself at the imp, wrapping her small
arms around his knees in a crushing embrace. Natterjack
rocked back in surprise, then reached down and very gently
patted her on the back with one big iron hand.

"How did you find me? I was worried. Did you wipe the
floor with those crines?"

"Honestly, you weren't that hard to find. To anyone who
can see magical traces, whatever happened here looks like
a bonfire. You're lucky that the Sisters haven't sent in a
fresh batch of minions yet or you'd be toast."

"How'd you get away from the crines?"

"That can wait a bit. First tell me...what happened
here?"

"There was a fairy here when the well creature attacked. She kept it from eating me. I don't know what happened to her after that."

Natterjack's eye widened. "You were attacked by the water wrath? And you survived. How'd you manage that?" He was genuinely shocked.

"It wasn't me, I don't think, it was mostly the fairy," she said.

"What...wait. You were fighting *with* the stickleback, not against?" Natterjack seemed truly surprised. "Listen, maybe you'd better tell me everything that happened after we were separated."

So she sat, gratefully gobbling at the canteen of water Natterjack shared with her, and told her whole tale. When she finished he shook his head in complete amazement. "I guess you're not as helpless as we both thought you were, are you?" he said, half smiling.

"I guess not," she said with a hint of pride. Her brow knitted. "But I really don't understand what it was that I did. Or if it really was me."

"Oh, I think it was you, all right," Natterjack said. "We already knew that you were special because the Witches wanted you and you learned Impish just by being near me. Now we know that you can not only speak Impish, but also Fairy. Not to mention the most extraordinary part—that you can channel Deep Magic."

"Is that what it's called?" she asked.

"Deep, Ancient, Archaic, Old Form, First Form are just

a few of the names used to describe the kind of magic that you tapped into. It's incredibly powerful and incredibly dangerous, but one thing is for sure. We can't stay here much longer. Not in this spot. The afterimage is like a beacon and it will be hot for hours."

"First Form?" she said, staring down in thought. "That sounds so familiar." But the memory, if that's what it was, wouldn't come to her. After a moment she gave up on it and her thoughts turned toward the things she had learned in his absence. "Jack," she began quietly. "When we first met I asked you how big the Kitchen was and you said I wouldn't believe you if you told me."

"I remember."

"It doesn't end, does it? It just keeps going on, and it keeps shifting and changing forever," she asked.

"No." Natterjack shook his head slowly. "It doesn't end...but there are some places that stay pretty much in the same area that you leave them, and only one place that absolutely doesn't move. Guthrie. If you stay in the Kitchen long enough, you get used to it and you learn how to find your way around by general landmarks and by being sensitive to the magic that is at work, but there's no guarantee that you'll see the same place twice."

"Jack, I don't want to stay here even if we find out what the Witches want from me, but...I don't know how we'll ever find our way out of a place like this, honestly."

"Listen, you should know by now that things are not

that simple in the Kitchen. Listen carefully to what I'm about to say, all right?"

She nodded.

"The Kitchen is vast. It is truly a world unto itself. But you have to understand that you are never very far from the outside world. That's kind of horrible in a way, but it's also a little bit comforting. The Kitchen is like a bubble that floats up next to another bubble and where they touch, they join. Yes, you could spend forever in the Kitchen and never find the front door, but that doesn't mean we can't find a way to get you out. The front door isn't the only door. Is it easy? No. But more than how we get out, we need to get back your memory. A journey of a thousand stone starts with the first step, right? Let's start there—don't get too far ahead of ourselves. That's what you want, right? Your memory?"

The tears in her eyes were enough of an answer for Natterjack. "Well, okay then. We know what we need to know: that Witches and Kitchen be damned."

She nodded, head down, and said, "You're the only friend I have, Jack."

Natterjack shook his head and said, "I don't think that's entirely accurate." He was looking over her shoulder at something and she turned to see what it was.

The tiny fairy stood about four hops away and she had her swords in her hands. She said in that melodic, barely audible flutelike voice, *Siri misir Impi nerei Kethish?*

"I don't speak Fairy. What did she say?" asked Natterjack.

The Toad translated, looking rather confused, "She's asking if you are turning Keth or do you remain Impish?" Then she added, "I don't get it. I don't know what she means."

Natterjack winced at the question, "Tell her I am Impish. I will not turn."

The Toad translated, then under her breath so that only Natterjack could hear, "What's Keth?"

"Later. I'll tell you later," he replied.

The fairy seemed to grow a bit agitated and said, "Prove it, show me your eyes." The Toad translated but it was plainly obvious to her that Natterjack had only one eye.

Natterjack stood and slowly he reached up and removed his knitted cap. Underneath, one above the other, two more eyes became visible. The lids fluttered and they blinked open. They were both the same sparkling shade of green as his first eye.

The Toad gasped. "Why do you keep them covered?"

"It's a long story. I'll tell you but not right now," he said, not taking his eyes off the fairy.

The fairy leaned forward, squinting at him. She nodded slowly and after a long pause strapped her swords onto her back. She walked up to about half a hop away and just stood there with arms folded, an unreadable expression on her pointed little face.

"I don't think she likes you much," the Toad said to Natterjack.

"Imps and sticklebacks do not get along very well," he said, then added, "but she's not just a stickleback, she's a sylphur."

"What's a sylphur?" the Toad asked.

"A stickleback, which if you haven't guessed, is the Kitchen's twisted version of a regular fairy. Sylphurs have been cast out by their tribe, usually because they break the hierarchy and do their own thing. Those swords were her wings, until she left her brood. She needs them because without some sort of weapon she will be defenseless when the rest of her tribe begins to hunt her for food, which they will eventually do."

"That's horrible!" the Toad exclaimed. "They wouldn't really eat her, would they?"

Natterjack paused for a moment. "Sticklebacks are brutal in general, and even more so to one who has been cast out. But with those blades for defense she's well equipped to handle herself," he continued, wanting to alleviate the worry that he saw in the Toad's eyes. "Besides, the sticklebacks won't attack us if we stick together. They might see us, but they'll certainly leave us be."

"I guess she's alone, too, then." The Toad looked back at the fairy, who regarded them in stoic silence. "Just like I was."

CHAPTER FOURTEEN

t's **time to go.** Not only will the Sisters be able to find us if we stay here, but anything else of power will, as well." Suddenly the fairy, who had resumed keeping her distance from Jack, strode over and positioned herself beside the Toad, making eye contact with the imp.

"If we travel, travel now, yes," said the Toad, translating as the fairy spoke.

Natterjack snapped his fingers, inspired. The fairy took a step back and placed a hand on one of her swords. He chuckled at her. "Ask her if she can see the path to...crap. What do the sticklebacks call it? Still...StillBright Hollow!"

Translating for Jack and the fairy, Toad said, "She says she was near there this morning, and it's not but four hundred stone away." The Toad's heart leaped in her chest.

"Really?! That's great!" She paused. "Wait. How far is four hundred stone?"

Natterjack pointed to the floor and counted, "One stone, two stone. Get it? Still, though, it could take some time to find it. The distance between might have changed."

The Toad asked the fairy, "Can you find StillBright Hollow?"

The fairy looked at them with a slightly crooked smile on her face, said "eh," spun on her heels, and began to walk quickly away.

"She said yes! I guess we should be following," the Toad said as Jack grabbed his pack and started after her, hustling to catch up.

Natterjack mused to the Toad, "Fairies are, in part, made of the magic of the area that they live in. I'd wager the Kitchen isn't as confusing to her as it is to us."

A few paces down the path the party lapsed into silence. While there was some safety in numbers, it was still wise to make as little noise as possible.

They had been walking for quite some time when the Toad noticed Jack stiffen suddenly.

She looked up at Jack and mouthed, "What's going on?"

In a very low voice Natterjack said, "We're being followed on three sides—the left, the right, and behind—by some...things, there are more than three. Keep calm. For whatever reason, they're only following. They're not trying to cut us off and they're not getting any closer."

She discreetly looked around. Whatever was keeping pace with them must have been doing it outside the sphere of her vision; she saw no signs of movement at all. Once or twice she saw what could have been a shifting shadow but it was so subtle she couldn't be sure.

"We should tell the fairy," she whispered to Jack.

"She knows," he replied. "She knew before I did. I saw her loosen the straps on her blades. That's what made me think that something was up. She doesn't seem too tense about it yet, though. Whatever's out there might just be curious about our little group."

"Let's hope," she said.

They had walked on for fifty or so paces when Natterjack looked up and said, "Hell. Where's the fairy?"

As they stood looking for her, they heard muffled thumps and rustles work their way around first to their right, then behind, then the left, then in front of them. The last one sounded briefly like a squealing pig but it ceased almost as soon as it began.

They tensed, waiting for an attack of some kind, but

they were met with silence. From the darkness ahead, the fairy appeared, striding back to the Toad and Jack. She was dragging a larger bound creature behind her.

The head of the beast, and beastly is what it appeared to be, turned toward the group. It had no eyes, but it did have huge, batlike ears and a full set of very wicked-looking fangs in a thickly muscled jaw. The fairy had done an excellent job of securing the beast; a portion of the braided fairy cord passed around its bulbous head and through its mouth, like the bit of a horse. Though it emitted a low barrel-chested growl, the binding kept it mostly silent. It most resembled a large, densely muscled bat. The Toad thought it looked flightless but still had membranous skin, folded between its limbs.

"Ugh! Does it always drool like that?" The Toad inched away from the viscous puddle slowly forming under the thing's head.

"Ig-trolls. Yeah, they do that. The fairy braid doesn't help," Natterjack said matter-of-factly, kneeling down to examine the catch. "Can you ask how many there are? These things usually run in herds."

"She says there were four. She chased three of them away and caught this one because..." She turned back to the fairy, who said, *"Evari dismai,"* and pointed at the struggling ig-troll.

The Toad took a half step back, a look of revulsion on her face. "That is not right. Jack, that fairy is just...

I mean, YUCK! What is wrong with her?"

"What did she say?" Jack said, looking more closely at the creature.

"She said, 'Good eating'! Can you believe that?"

Natterjack paused for a moment and looked up from the ground near the ig-troll. With a very innocent smile he raised his eyebrow and said, "So you don't want any, then?"

"Okay, it's like this: Fairy light does not radiate heat and fairy fire does not radiate light," Natterjack explained as they sat around their makeshift campfire. Only there was no fire at the center of their circle, at least no regular fire, only a shimmering undulation, hovering just off the ground. After they decided to stop, rest, and eat, the fairy walked over to the middle of their group and made a small intricate gesture with her hands. The wavering fairy fire rippled into existence almost at once. Above it she constructed a spit made from collected sticks, twigs, and a few pieces of tarnished dinnerware.

The feral creature was struggling ferociously against its restraints and if it had been anything other than magical fairy braid, it would have chewed through long ago. All the preparations made the Toad morose and uncomfortable.

"Everything eats something," Natterjack said. "Most things would eat you if given half the chance."

"That doesn't make me feel any better at all. I mean... what if these creatures..." She had started to say "could talk" but stopped herself. It occurred to her that they probably could talk to each other. After all, she was a toad and she could speak, and plenty of things had wanted to eat her. Natterjack had said he could speak most animal tongues, too, but he was still okay with eating the ig-troll. She just didn't think he'd understand. Regardless, she didn't like the idea of eating a thinking, talking creature.

Natterjack read her expression. "It's not like that. Look, it's nature. It's natural. It is survival. Everything eats something living. Some animals eat meat, others are vegetarian."

"Well, at least vegetables don't talk or have feelings," she said emphatically.

Jack interjected, "That's not really true. There are places in the Kitchen where the plants won't stop talking.

If you stand around and listen to them, they just prattle on endlessly about this and that."

"Yes, but the Kitchen is different. There are different rules here." She paused, realizing what she had just said.

If I'm from the Kitchen, then how did I know it was different? Different from what? Her mind strained at the thought, trying to discover the hint of memory that had spawned it, but once again it was useless.

"That's the point," said Natterjack. "The Kitchen requires that you do what it takes to survive. If you don't, then you don't. It's as simple as that." He smiled gently. "The key is to refrain from establishing an ongoing relationship with your food."

"And speaking of meat eaters, where has the stickleback gone?" the Toad asked. The little group had taken to keeping track of one another, even the fairy, who was making a habit of vanishing and reappearing at will. When the Toad asked Jack if the fairy was using some sort of magic to do this he just shook his head and said, "She's just sneaky, that one."

Even though the idea of eating the ig-troll repulsed her, the notion of food had awakened her appetite and her thirst. "How do we find water?"

Jack laughed and replied, "Every kitchen has a sink, and a kitchen this big has many, and more than one well. It's easy enough when you have a nose for it, which you obviously do."

The Toad was still considering this when a bundle landed on the floor in front of her.

She looked up and saw that the fairy had returned. She shifted her gaze back to the floor and said with more than a little apprehension, "Um. I'm kind of afraid to ask, what's this?" She poked at the bundle and realized that it was made of three or four large leaves, bound in twine, wrapped around something. Whatever it was, it wasn't moving. "What have you killed now?"

The fairy stepped back, crossing her arms, shaking her head, and rolling her eyes in an overly dramatic fashion. She pointed at the bundle and said, "Eat now . . . eat, eat."

The Toad prodded at the bundle until it came undone, spilling its bright red contents on the floor. The fairy had brought her berries.

The Toad looked up at Jack, then over at the struggling ig-troll.

"Can't we just let it go? Aren't there enough berries for all of us?" she said earnestly, though the pile looked meager next to her hunger.

"Look, you've got to understand that we all have to eat and not everyone eats berries." On cue, the fairy walked over to the ig-troll and began to unbuckle one of her swords.

"Stop!" the Toad rose to her full height, but the fairy just shook her head and drew her sword.

"Don't you do it!" She lurched forward a half step.

The fairy's eyes narrowed as she raised the blade.

She kept her eyes on the fairy. "You are not going to kill him!"

As she yelled, the Toad began to shift colors again, but this time it was different. Instead of aquas and lavenders, she shifted greyish green to midnight blue to crimson. There was no immense thunderclap, no flash or prismatic lightning, no sound at all. Until the fairy began to shriek.

Just as the fairy's blade would have made contact with the thick neck of the ig-troll, it vanished right out of her hand. It wasn't the only thing to have disappeared. The fairy braid that had been binding the creature was gone.

The fairy screeched as the beast leaped up and lashed out, catching the fairy completely by surprise. It landed on her with all its force, knocking her flat on her back and pinning her down with stubby clawed forepaws. It opened its massive maw, flexing its jaw and showing its huge fangs. The fairy struggled beneath the beast. She was very strong for her size, but she was not as strong as the ig-troll. Her speed could not help her, prone as she was, and her last remaining blade was still buckled to her back. She was helpless.

"*Chhhhiirrrrrooopppp!!!*" A piercing whistle broke through the air, like a click and a high-pitched whistle joined into one.

It had an astonishing effect on the ig-troll. The creature stepped off the fairy, backed up, and sat down on the floor like an obedient dog, head cocked to one side, listening with its huge bat ears.

The Toad continued making the strange sounds. The ig-troll stood up and padded over to her. Timidly, it stretched its nose out and sniffed the air. She lifted her hand and fearlessly placed it on the creature's forehead. The beast sniffed at her forearm, wheeled, and bounded off into the darkness.

The Toad's colors stopped shifting at that moment and she sat down, staring at the floor, waiting for someone to yell at her for what she'd done. She knew it wasn't right, but she couldn't stop herself. Killing the ig-troll wasn't right, either.

The fairy was nowhere to be seen, and Jack asked, "What did you do to it? The sword, I mean."

"I don't know what I did. I just wanted it gone before she hurt the troll. Why?"

"Deep Magic is powerful and strange. If you didn't actually intend to destroy the blade, you might be able to get it back."

"Really?"

"Depends on you," Jack said.

Her hunger was gone, replaced by a tight knot of tension. She wasn't sorry about the troll but she felt horrible about the fairy. The fairy had been constantly, inexplicably helping her, even brought her the berries because she wouldn't eat the troll. And the Toad had repaid her by almost getting her killed and taking what was one of the only two things in the world that the sylphur valued. The other, of course, being the second sword.

I didn't ask for her help, the Toad thought. But truthfully, she had accepted it, almost at once. *It's one thing to fight and defend yourself but the ig-troll had just been following us like... like a curious puppy. I don't even think it was going to attack us. But I still wish... No, I want to get her sword back.*

"Jack, do you think she's gone for good?" she asked.

"Nope," the imp said simply.

"How do you know?"

He pointed. "She's standing over there."

The Toad instantly saw the small lithe silhouette of the fairy. She looked strange with only one sword strapped to her back. "I have to talk to her."

"That might not be safe, Toad. She still has one blade and we know how fast she is when she wants to be."

"I have to," she replied softly. As the Toad neared her it became obvious that she wasn't going to run away or attack. She was crying. Her hands covered her face and her tears made sparkling streaks that ran between her fingers.

The fairy sensed the Toad's presence and began to speak in a trembling, softly fluting voice, what sounded like, "Mercy, for the blade... mercy."

The Toad didn't understand. She began to ask but stopped as the fairy looked at her from between her hands. Her expression was not forlorn. It was cold and calculating.

The Toad suddenly realized what the fairy had been saying. She wasn't begging for mercy. She had been

90

saying, "Mercy, for the blade I will give you mercy." But her understanding came just a moment too late.

The Toad didn't even have time to croak. The fairy moved blindingly fast and was standing at her side, with her sword at the Toad's soft white throat.

The fairy spoke again. She repeated, "I will give you mercy for the blade."

CHAPTER FIFTEEN

I can't, I don't know how," the Toad said to the fairy.

The fairy's grip tightened and the blade pressed firmly against the thin skin on the underside of her chin.

"Give me what is mine and I will let you keep what is yours," the fairy said.

Strangely, the Toad did not feel frightened or angry at being held hostage; she was concerned and frustrated at her own stupidity. She really did want to return the sword to the fairy, but up to this point all of the magic that she had done had either been subconscious or accidental.

"I don't know what I'm doing, I don't even know how I made it disappear," the Toad said in the melodic fairy tongue.

"Learn," the fairy said simply. "Or die. Your magic is a sword, and you are careless with it."

"I was protecting the troll. I asked you to stop!"

"You did not ask. You commanded. But I am what I am because I have to be. I do not kill out of cruelty. I kill out of necessity. Fairies in the Kitchen do not eat plants. You cannot change that. It is not your decision. I will not starve to death because of your childishness."

The fairy's grip had relaxed, but the Toad made no attempt to escape. She knew that she was in danger, but she also wanted to fix this problem. "I have no control over this power. It just comes out of me and things happen."

"You intended to stop me; don't deny that. This power doesn't come out of you. It isn't its own. It is you. You cause things to happen when you lose control of yourself. I suffer because you can't direct your intentions. My weapons are an extension of myself, as are yours." She paused, then added, "If I were like the others of my kind you'd already be dead for what you've done. You live because I have mercy. I've watched you and you don't yet know yourself.

Magic is a new discovery to you and in you it's wild. I won't suffer further for your lack of understanding."

"You know magic. You could show me how to use it," the Toad said.

"No," the fairy said flatly.

"Why not?"

"I cannot teach you magic. You have a different power than I." The fairy paused. "But I can teach you to control yourself." She released the Toad and stepped back.

"I promise I will get your sword back," the Toad said as she rubbed the spot on her neck where the sword had been.

The fairy lifted the sword and pointed at the Toad. "You for yours, me for mine, yes; but not in payment, not in exchange. You return my sword because you shouldn't have taken it and I teach you because I can."

The Toad looked up at her. "Yes. I am sorry. I meant no..."

"If I thought you intended me harm I would not be here," the fairy said. "And neither would you."

It occurred to the Toad that she hadn't asked the fairy her name. Considering that they had just had their first fight it seemed proper that they should be on a first-name basis. Of course the Toad didn't know her own name, still... "What are you called?"

"No one calls me," the fairy said plainly.

"But if they did, what would they...I mean, what is your name?"

The fairy looked at her solemnly and answered, "I am Horsefly."

The Toad said, "I don't know my name; I can't remember."

"When you know yourself, you will know your name. I will call you Leaper till then," Horsefly said with a nod.

The Toad wanted to thank Horsefly. She was glad to reach a resolution, learn from her, and know her name, and felt that something had been strengthened between them. But try as she might, it seemed that there were no words in the fairy language that would express her feelings. In a flash of insight she understood. Fairies did not thank each other . . . ever. None of them ever felt thankful.

Jack sat looking over at the Toad and the fairy. They had been talking continuously since the fairy had released the Toad.

"Ahem. Pardon us, please," a voice issued from the darkness.

Jack was on his feet and next to the Toad in an instant. The fairy was suddenly nowhere to be seen.

"Name yourselves," Jack said, his hands balled into iron fists. "Name yourselves as decent Wickerfolk or do yourselves a favor and leave us be."

After a moment of tense silence two small shapes stepped out from behind a large wooden crate.

"Pug and Sootfoot, travelers and Wickers. We are on our way to Guthrie's break by way of the silent path and then on to our hearths and homes."

They were both about three hands high, human hands, that is. The one named Pug was built like a tiny man, relatively speaking, and he was aptly named. To describe him as "brickish" one might well have to redefine bricks as being quite a bit wider. "Squarish" was more like it. While he had no hair on his head he more than made up for it with an enormous braided mustache and beard.

They both carried brown leather traveling bags, but the other, the one called Sootfoot, otherwise wore no clothes at all. He was covered all over in fine brown and white fur. He stood upright, but had a pair of jack legs ending in two dark fur-covered paws, and his face tapered back into long, soft, pointed ears on either side of his sparkling green

eyes. He looked to be half man, half fox. He was holding a flute in his hand.

"Did ya know yer traveling with a stickleback? That's a bit odd," said Pug.

Jack half-smiled and unclenched his fists. "The stickleback's our guide. She's much easier to follow than the silent path. We're headed to the break as well. You're welcome to travel with us for as long as you're able."

Sootfoot bowed and said, "We're sorry to have frightened her off, but one can't be too careful."

"Oh, you didn't frighten her," Jack said, making a point of looking past the two characters.

Pug and Sootfoot followed Jack's gaze and almost yelped in unison when they saw the fairy not a stone away with her sword drawn on them.

The Toad said something in Fairy and Horsefly stepped away, simultaneously securing her sword to her back.

"You have been deemed safe, it would seem," Jack said. "Come and sit."

They sat around the fairy fire and grew acquainted, at least as much as their hushed con-versations would allow.

"You should know," Jack began, "the Witches are after us and they've set the crines on our trail."

Sootfoot's brow narrowed and Pug's eyes opened wide in surprise.

"Umm, maybe we shouldn't be, uh...Soot," Pug started, "should we get inta this? I mean the Witches are..."

"...always after someone," Sootfoot finished. "Calm down. There are thousands of ways to catch your end in the Kitchen. You know as well as I that the Kitchen keeps its own very well hidden. I say we have a better chance of finding Guthrie if we stick together. We are Wickerfolk after all. We help each other when we can."

Never without a question, the Toad asked, "What are Wickerfolk?"

Wickerfolk was a name that, as Sootfoot explained it, described the various denizens of the Kitchen with social inclinations. This technically included some of the more dangerous and bloodthirsty creatures, but usually Wickerfolk were of good nature and sought some form of community.

"How can the Wickerfolk have a community here? You can't be sure of this place from one moment to the next," the Toad whispered.

"Well, isn't it obvious? We commune with any and all creatures that don't immediately try to consume us." Sootfoot smiled broadly and gave a quick glance to Natterjack, who merely murmured, "True, true.

"Speaking of communing, are you and the fairy settled?" Jack asked, speaking discreetly to the Toad.

"Yes," the Toad whispered, "at least we understand each other better."

"I was worried about you. I knew I couldn't get between you, but I wasn't sure what she'd do. Looks like she was just trying to get your attention."

"It worked, I guess."

"But you two look tied faster than before. Sometimes a good fight between friends can make all the difference in the world. I was wrong about that stickleback. She's cut of a different cloth. Where has she gone?"

"Hunting," the Toad said, looking down. "I asked her to bring food back for you." She looked up at Jack. "I shouldn't have done what I did. I just couldn't stand thinking about the troll being killed and eaten. I've been running from, or fighting off, things that have wanted to kill or eat me since I woke up in here and I guess I felt sorry for it. I knew what it felt like. It was alone and helpless like I was before I met you."

Jack said, "Helpless is something you are definitely not, not anymore anyway. You probably never were. The Witches want you because of your abilities. It's what they do. They steal the talents of others and you definitely have something they want. I think it's time to find out how special you really are. When the fairy gets back we should get going as soon as we can."

When Horsefly returned she carried four leaf-wrapped bundles. She gave the Toad her bundle first and said, "Eat away from the others."

The Toad walked a few paces away as the others began to unwrap and cook the meat that the fairy had given them. She unwrapped her bundle and made short work of the assorted berries and leaves inside. It was a quiet, uncomfortable meal and she felt isolated from her new friends, but in the end everyone was well fed and the Toad's hunger was finally satisfied. The berries were so juicy her thirst was abated as well.

"Aren't you going to eat?" she asked Horsefly.

"I eat where I kill. The warmth of the animal still resides in the flesh," Horsefly said plainly.

"I didn't need to know that," the Toad said, a sour look on her face.

The fairy merely smiled at her and shrugged.

"You're not going to make this easy for me, are you?" The Toad sighed.

"Easy? What is easy? It is time to leave."

The group gathered their few belongings as Horsefly gestured with her hand, extinguishing the wavering, invisible fire.

They began to walk. This time the silence seemed deeper than before.

CHAPTER SIXTEEN

he study was dim and quiet, broken only by Emilina's distracted leafing through an old tome of archaic alphabets, a small trembling deimus light floating over her shoulder. She looked at the yellowed pages as she thumbed through the book but she wasn't really seeing what was written on the aged parchment. It had been a very long time since she had read any book other than the dark Book. There were very few problems that the Book could not solve. There were very few questions that it could not answer. It would show her how to find the Toad.

Emilina's impassive face twitched at the thought of the missing amphibian. She could barely contain the seething rage and frustration that was welling up inside her. The thin witch would control herself, though—she had to—because these emotions would block her communication with the Book and that would not do, not do at all.

Sarafina sat across from her sister and could sense Emilina's mood. She knew that the worst thing she could do at this moment was to try to speak to her sister. At the best of times Emilina would only barely tolerate Sarafina's awkward attempts at conversation and now...well, this was far from the best of times. Indeed it had been Sarafina's "pet" that had caused all of this, but how could she have known that the little creeping crib would misbehave in such a manner? It had never acted *that* strangely, not for a reanimated dead bird, that is. Why had it been hostile toward her? She had given it the black marble that restored its partial life. That, in and of itself, was normally enough to elicit complete control over a crib or a crine, and crines were much more powerful. Sarafina thought back to the day that she had found this particular crib. She had collected the skeleton in the forest. She liked to use birds rather than any other animal because they were the most numerous and the easiest to rise up. Their small forms took very little power to animate.

She remembered that she had acquired five that day. She found this particular bird, a small kestrel falcon, in its nest lying next to a silver-tipped shortbow arrow. The skeleton had been pristine, except for the small notch in its side where the arrow had felled it. Sarafina had marveled at its tragic beauty and at its strength. How it must have struggled to return to its nest with an arrow in its side, and now its tiny, pale skeleton was seated in the perfectly woven and immaculate structure. It looked as though it had fallen asleep with its little head tucked under its wing.

She had brought all of them, along with the beautiful nest, to her room and begun the process of animation. She had to start by snapping off the bony wing tips of each bird, though it seemed a shame to ruin this one beautiful specimen. This was the first step in reanimating any bird-based cribs, because if they were raised with their full wing bones intact then they were always trying to fly and flit about. Cribs with full wings wouldn't get anything done. Next, a small black stone marble was placed in one of its eye sockets and magical words of investment were spoken. Finally, they were wrapped in thin gauze and left overnight, soaking in a shallow bowl of milk taken from a deceased cow. They would awaken when the gauze was removed, ready to perform whatever duties the Sisters assigned to them, which usually amounted to spying, stealing, and light cleaning around the keep.

After the awakening ritual was performed, this particular little creature seemed normal enough, for a crib. But slowly in the days that followed, Sarafina had noticed that it was acting oddly, but in harmless ways. It seemed that no matter where she would station the crib it wouldn't stay put. More than that, it followed her. On more than one occasion Sarafina would be performing a ritual and turn to find the little crib right behind her or on a shelf staring at her. Emilina noticed this almost at once and commanded

Sarafina to destroy the whole batch of cribs, accusing Sarafina of making some grievous error in their creation. Which was completely unfair, considering that where magic was concerned, Sarafina was as accomplished as she was large. She never, ever made mistakes in the application of magical energies. This was in fact one of the few things that the Sisters had in common.

After a time, to appease her sister, Sarafina did destroy the other cribs, but this one... well, it followed her and while it wouldn't be accurate to say that she had a soft spot for small animals you could say that she had a slightly less hard spot for this little bird thing. She had taken to keeping the crib in her room, mostly to keep Emilina from finding out that she hadn't done as she was told. It had certainly been a mistake in the end but there was another aspect of the situation that troubled Sarafina as much as the crib's attack: How had it gotten out of her room—and how had it gotten into the Kitchen?

"Tha criness are scratching at the dooorrah," the demon Grisswell spoke into the silence of the room.

Sarafina, startled, nearly fell backward out of her chair. The demon did not present itself to the mortal plane unless called for a specific purpose and she had never quite gotten used to his growling voice sounding out of nowhere and without warning.

"Grisswell, why are you here? Did I not instruct you to let the crines out after we released them into the Kitchen?" Emilina's voice was calm, smooth, and full of menace.

"Yesa, sister, thee did instruct me thus. I haff opened tha dooor, but they cannot come," he replied.

"Why not?" she asked.

There was no answer.

"Grisswell...WHY NOT?"

"They are diiiieiing."

"Did he say they are dying?" Sarafina stuttered.

"Be quiet!" Emilina snapped. "Grisswell, seal the door and bring them here!"

"Yeasah, Sister." And with that his voice faded.

"How can they be...they can't be dying! They can't be killed, not by anything less than a demon, and there aren't any demons in the kitchen!" Sarafina exclaimed.

There was a loud, sizzling crackle as an elongated twisting shadow became visible over the table. Issuing from its heart poured a shuddering, coagulated assemblage of bones. Smoldering, they spilled out onto the table in a fused and barely recognizable mess. Only one of the creatures was still barely alive, its clawed foot opening and closing slowly, carving deep gouges into the wood.

Sarafina bolted to her feet and stood looking at the pile of smoking bones with an expression of astonishment on her mottled face.

Emilina sat with her fingers laced together in front of her and her brow furrowed in deep contemplation. She spoke a single word of magic and the last living crine stopped moving. She stared at the new claw marks in the dark wood of the table and after a moment she looked up into

Sarafina's eyes. It was a rare moment when both Sisters had the same thought at the same time and this was one of those moments. They looked at each other, then said in unison:

"Natterjack."

CHAPTER SEVENTEEN

Well..." Sootfoot offered. "My best guess puts us within two hundred stone of Guthrie's break." He was attempting to buffer the quiet that had settled among them, but was unsuccessful. Everyone had withdrawn into their own thoughts.

"I think we may be a bit closer than that," Natterjack said. "It seems to me that the Kitchen has become almost motionless now and you know that the closer we get to Guthrie the more stable the environment becomes."

The Toad interjected, "So how would we stay on the path? I mean, if the fairy wasn't here to lead us, if she had left. The Kitchen isn't moving. It's all quiet."

Jack said, "Well, once you hit this part, you just keep moving toward the center. It gets easier actually, and when we're within ten stone we should be able to see Guthrie's light."

"Is that why the fairies call it StillBright Hollow? Because there's daylight there?" the Toad asked.

"It's light, but it's not daylight. Actually, it really isn't all that bright, either," Jack replied. "Don't get the idea that it's not dangerous, though. There are many things that hunt outside the break, simply because it's easier to spot prey. Remember, Guthrie is not our destination; it's a landmark that will hopefully make it easier to find the Widows."

"I know, I know," she said, but in truth she had been so focused on finding Guthrie that she had forgotten that they were actually looking for the Widows of the Clock. Her heart sank a little.

"Gaw! Yer goin' ta see th' Widows?" Pug questioned. "They're an unpleasant lot, so I've heard. The stories about them kinda creep me out."

"Yeah, unpleasant," the Toad said, watching Pug jam a thick finger into his ear and twirl it.

In the midst of their discussion, the fairy walked back and stood, arms folded in front of her chest, and began tapping her foot.

"I believe that is an indication that we are lollygagging," said Sootfoot.

They picked up their pace and the Toad kept her eyes glued to the fairy, constantly looking for any sign that something might be amiss. On more than one occasion

Horsefly paused and put her hand on her sword hilt before continuing on. The Kitchen seemed to have stopped moving altogether and this made the Toad's heart begin to race with excitement. After what seemed like a very long time she began to notice a slight glow in front of them. She clutched at Natterjack's pant leg and looked at him with a questioning expression. *Is this it?*

To his credit, it couldn't be the easiest thing in the world to read the expression on a toad's face. But he understood, and nodded to her. She almost leaped ahead in her excitement, but the fairy put out her hand and gave her a harsh look that stopped her in her tracks. The fairy pointed to her ear.

The Toad stopped and closed her eyes. It was a moment before she heard it. She thought that they must have gotten turned around because it sounded like the low shuffling of the Kitchen again. But that couldn't be—she still saw Guthrie's light.

They quietly came to an immense china cabinet. Jack crept up next to the fairy and stole a quick glance around it. The Toad saw his face tense and his brow furrow. He glanced at her and said in a low whisper, "Look fast."

Staying as low to the floor as she could, she peeked around the corner, then quickly withdrew.

The area on the other side was glowing with a soft blue light. Jack had been right, they couldn't be ten stone away from what must be Ol' Guthrie's place.

All they had to do now was get past the hundred or so crines that were surrounding it.

"There is no way I can handle that many," Jack whispered. "I don't understand how they made so many so quickly. It only takes a day or so to make a crib, but a crine has to be grown over a few weeks. I have no idea how long it takes to make the altered ones, and I saw at least seven of those. The Witches must have found a new recipe in that damned book of theirs."

The small band of travelers had drawn back to a safer distance, well away from the enormous china cabinet that blocked them from the black, searching eyes of the many skeletal birdlike creatures. They were drawn close together, even the fairy, because none of them would venture a sound above a quiet whisper.

"What do we do?" the Toad asked. "How are we going to get past those things? I mean, do we have to go into Guthrie's place? Can't we just circle around it and still find our way? We only needed it as a landmark, right?"

"It doesn't work like that," Jack stated with a heavy sigh. "I wish it did, but you have to enter the still point, then step out again in the direction you intend to go. If you do that, you'll be headed on the right course."

"I could try this." Sootfoot held up his flute. "It's a spiralsong flute. If I get it right, its magic could incapacitate the creatures."

"No offense, but a spiralsong is low magic. Even if you

were an expert in the playing of that flute it would never affect more than a handful."

Sootfoot slumped visibly. "No offense taken; you are quite right."

"Fine, then what are we going to do?" The Toad tried not to sound as frustrated and worried as she really was.

"Thas' a good question," Pug interjected. "And another is, how did those bone birds figure out where we was headin'? Did ole Broom Head and Bull Britches set them to guard against us?"

"If you mean the Sisters, then, yes, I most certainly believe they set the crines against us, specifically against the Toad here. But as to how they knew where we were going, that is a bit of a mystery."

Horsefly leaned over and whispered into the Toad's ear. After a few minutes of disagreeing and discussing, the Toad turned to the group. "The fairy has a plan," the Toad said hesitantly. "I don't like it, but it could work...I think."

"Listen, following a stickleback around the Kitchen is one thing..." Pug said. "But are we sure we wanna be trustin' our lives ta her?"

"Her name is Horsefly. She's the reason we're not going

hungry, and if you don't trust her by now, Pug...well, I'd like you to stay but you don't have to," the Toad said.

Pug looked at Sootfoot, who merely raised his eyebrows and shrugged, saying, "If we can't get to Guthrie, we can't find our village. Who knows how long the Witches will sit the crines around the break. We should hear her out at least. We've come this far."

Jack looked at the small group, his eye coming to rest on the fairy. "She's proven her worth as well as or better than any here. Tell us Horsefly's plan."

CHAPTER EIGHTEEN

atterjack **smiled.** It was a great plan, in theory. The fairy, inspired by their recent encounter with the ig-trolls, suggested a strategy that seemed simple, sound, and plausible given the relatively low intelligence of the feral crines. Even taking into account the smarter, altered crines, it could work. The fairy would find a small group of ig-trolls and the Toad would command them to sprint past the skeletal guards, causing a brief distraction that would allow the small band of travelers to sneak into Guthrie's break unnoticed. The brilliant part was that Natterjack would make the ig-trolls appear as the band of companions, and conversely the companions would be made to appear as the ig-trolls. The Toad balked at using the trolls as bait but calmed when the fairy told her about the ig-trolls' extraordinary speed.

Their vestigial wing membranes gave them the ability to hop and glide for short distances, which was why they were usually so dangerous and difficult to catch.

"I've never heard of such a thing, trying to trick crines with glamour. Is it even possible?" Sootfoot asked incredulously.

"It ain't, I say," Pug said, shaking his head.

Nonetheless, he, the Toad, Sootfoot, and Horsefly looked at Jack for a deciding opinion.

Jack said, "And you'd be okay with this?"

The Toad looked down at the floor thoughtfully. "If you think it would work. I don't like it, but I guess I could live with it."

"Ha! I think it could work," he said, looking back at the fairy, who gave him a wink with her most mischievous smile.

"In fact, I think it's a damn good idea, if we can find some igs."

"She already knows where they are, remember. She went hunting," the Toad said somberly.

"I guess we're set. Let's get to it, then," Jack said.

Horsefly, accompanied by the Toad, backtracked and quickly relocated the herd of ig-trolls. In short order she spotted an isolated group of five. They were of various sizes; the largest was nearly as big as Natterjack. Horsefly crept up behind the growling, snuffling creatures and began casting bursts of fairy fire around the small group, herding them toward the Toad.

As the Toad struggled to remember the trolls' language, the fairy steered one particularly large and vicious beast directly toward the Toad. The growling, grunting thing was only a few paces away when the Toad had a realization: *Wait! It isn't about words, it's about feeling!*

Just as the beast was about to spring on her, a short whistling, clicking sound barked out of the Toad's mouth.

"TTHHHIIIRRRRRRPPP!"

The ig-troll pulled up short and slid to a stop mere inches away from her, its head cocked at a curious angle, listening.

She nailed it. The trolls had, at some point in this insane Kitchen, descended from bats. And although they had no audible language of their own they understood and responded to the strange batlike sounds on a primal level. All five of the creatures gathered together in a tight cluster, right in front of the Toad. A very small, wrinkled, and obviously ancient troll stepped forward and gave the air between them a good sniff. The Toad mentally named him Gristle. After another series of clicks and whistles, the Toad turned and began walking back toward Jack, Pug, and Sootfoot. The ig-trolls fell into a single line behind her with Gristle leading the rest. When she would hop, they would hop, keeping the distance between them constant. Horsefly walked beside her, but the trolls didn't even seem to notice that she was there. After a few moments they were back at their small camp, Natterjack standing at the ready, Pug and Sootfoot a safe distance away.

"Well done," Jack said. Gristle swiveled his head toward him and issued a deep, powerful growl. At once, the ig-trolls leaped and formed a line in front of the Toad. All of their heads were lowered and their daggerlike teeth were bared at the imp.

Four sharp clicks from the Toad and they all turned back toward her and sat down on the floor, instantly calm, every pair of large bat ears pointed directly at her.

Jack raised his eyebrow. "Wow. That's truly impressive." The only troll that paid any attention to him now was Gristle. One membranous ear swiveled toward Jack, then quickly back to the Toad.

"What did you say to them?" Jack asked.

"It's hard to explain. I mean, the sounds don't really translate into words," the Toad replied. "It's like I 'feel' at them and they respond similarly. Like this...watch..." The Toad paused, then issued a small, warbling whistle. Immediately the ig-trolls repositioned themselves on the floor front to back and began grooming each other with long, flat tongues.

"The sound that I made..." she said, "it made them feel the need to be close to each other. When I made it, I could feel it as well." She paused and looked up at Jack, her expression very serious. "Jack, I think I could make them do almost anything. They would fight for me if I wanted them to...to the death. I can feel it."

"Yeah, it looks that way." This time Jack paused. "You're worried that you might get them hurt or killed."

"Exactly," she said. "I can't be sure that I won't."

"No matter how much we plan, something could go wrong, Toad. But keep in mind, we suffer the same dangers as they do. We could end up worse off than them—they're much faster than we are. We'll do what we can to keep them safe and you can always make them run away if it gets too bad. That's really all we can do."

She took a deep breath. "I know. Okay...let's do this."

Jack began. It really didn't take long. As he worked on the first troll, the air around it shimmered, then coalesced into a transparent form that gradually became opaque. Standing in front of Jack was the perfect likeness of Horsefly, accurate in every detail. The Toad felt sad when she noticed that the imitation also had only one sword strapped to her back.

Each of the ig-trolls in turn became a member of their small party. The last and largest troll stared back with a replica of Jack's own big green eye.

"All right, now it's our turn," Jack said.

"Why is it," Sootfoot began, "that your magic isn't altered by the presence of the Toad?"

Jack stood in front of Pug, who had a distinctly sour look on his face, and began to gesture as he had with the ig-trolls, before answering Sootfoot's question. "The magic that I use is more powerful than the shallow magic of the Wickerfolk, so it's less likely to be influenced by outside energies. That doesn't mean she can't affect it, though."

Standing in front of Natterjack was a very squat, unhappy-looking creature. Pug raised his arm and flexed his stubby, clawed forepaw. "This ain't right. No sir, I don't like this one little bit."

"Calm down," Sootfoot said in his most soothing voice. "We need to get to Guthrie, Pug. Plus, it's not going to last very long, is it, Jack?"

"Long enough," he said, then added, "I hope."

"All right. Let's get this over with." He stepped in front of the Toad and began gesturing. The air around the Toad began shimmering as it had with the others but just as the shape began to form, it suddenly lost cohesion and dissipated as if blown apart by a strong wind. "Crap," Jack said. "I guess that answers our question."

"Can you try again?" the Toad asked.

"Yeah, I guess."

"Wait, let me try to relax," she said, glancing over at the fairy, who nodded her agreement. She closed her eyes. "Okay, I'm ready."

A few moments passed and though she felt nothing, she slowly opened her eyes. She raised her front leg to her face. It was covered in the wrinkled, leathery skin of an ig-troll. "That is...grotesque. I mean it's kinda cool, but creepy. I don't feel any different. Should I be able to feel it?"

"No," Jack said. "It's an illusion, a trick of the light, so to speak. You wouldn't feel it unless you actually changed shape into an ig-troll. And believe me, you wouldn't want to do that even if you could. Very dangerous stuff, shape changing. If you don't know what you're doing, you could lose yourself in another shape forever."

"Can you shape change?" she asked.

"Some imps can, to a degree, but not me. Let's finish this and get going."

A few moments later the small herd of "ig-trolls" began shepherding a small band of "traveling companions." As they neared the familiar china cabinet they could hear the low shuffling and clicking of the crines.

Jack whispered, "Okay, Toad, get them into position."

The Toad turned to the real trolls to give her instructions. She could sense their attention even through their bored illusory "faces."

Just as the trolls edged up to the passage around the cabinet, the imitation Sootfoot lowered his head and began to growl. From around the corner a small skeletal bird hopped into view. It looked at the Toad with its shiny, inscrutable black marble eye—not the ig-troll Toad but the

119

real Toad. It snapped its beak open and shut three times. *Click, click, click.* It sounded like the ticking of a watch, which was apt because the Toad had just enough time to say, "RUN!"

And then time ran out.

CHAPTER NINETEEN

t **hadn't worked.** Even before they could try, their plan was foiled. The creatures had gotten behind them, around them. There was nowhere to run. It was a trap.

There were crines everywhere. A heaving surge of living bones. No matter what direction the Toad turned, there they were, crouching and hissing. The skeletal birds undulated around them like a sea of snakes, and even still they were pouring over the dish cabinet and from the immediate darkness. The Toad and her friends were completely surrounded.

An altered crine landed directly in front of the still-disguised ig-trolls and when the cold blue light of its eye fell on them, the illusion broke. They huddled together, growling and barking at the crines.

The Toad spoke to them quickly. Gristle turned to her,

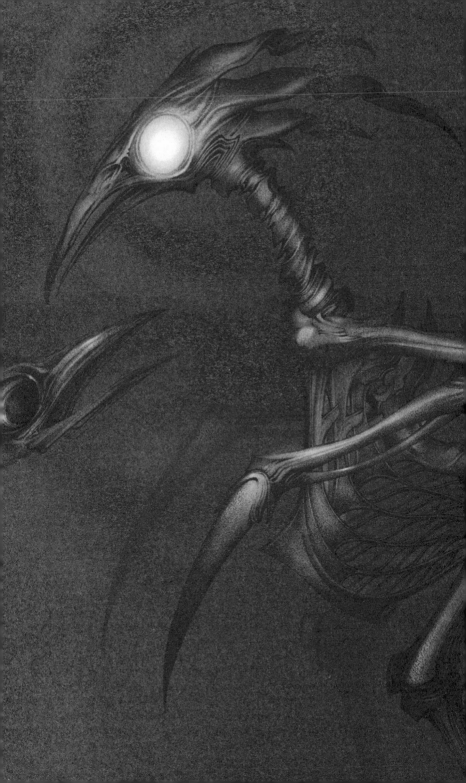

huge ears swiveling on his head, and in the next moment they were gone, even before the razor-sharp beaks of the crines stabbed at them. The crines bit empty air and stone floor. As fast as the skeletal birds were, the trolls were much, much faster. The batlike creatures scurried and hopped away at a dizzying speed. The Toad caught the briefest glimpse of Gristle's old and wrinkled butt as he leaped to a table leg, clung to it sideways, and then bolted out of sight.

"It won't be so easy for us," Jack said as the crines turned their full attention on the small herd of imitation trolls.

Now there were three altered crines bearing down on them. Again, as soon as the eye lights fell directly upon them, their disguises fell away. Except for the Toad. She looked down at her hands, fully expecting to see the familiar grey-green of her Toadish self. To her surprise, she still looked exactly like an ig-troll.

"Jack!" she started. "I'm still..."

"I know," he said in a low voice. "Don't speak at all. Act like a troll." She lowered her head and began to growl. It wasn't the deep, fierce growl of a troll, but it was close.

The crines were still circling their group. They seemed to be waiting for something. Four more altered creatures writhed their way into view. Now there were seven beams of blue light illuminating their tight circle.

"I can hear you...Jackal."

Jack's head snapped around but there was no one there, only the crines. "Great. You get a cookie," he said sarcastically. "Show yourself." His eye was wide and for the first time he looked afraid.

"Jack. It was the biggun," Pug shouted. "I saw it."

"Crines don't talk!" Jack said, shaking his head.

"Poor Jackal, all that knowledge and it doesn't help you." The voice was smooth and dripped menace. "I can do much more than speak."

The largest altered crine stepped forward. It began to grow taller and darker, its form shifting and squirming. It became a twisting column of pure black smoke that suddenly, silently exploded, leaving only a single figure standing where its center had been.

"Why, Jackal, it has been a long time, hasn't it? I do hope you've been doing well. How is the family?" Emilina smiled, but not at all sweetly.

"Liar. Your own face is ugly enough. I told you to show yourself," Jack said, his eye narrowing under a furrowed brow. Behind him Pug had fainted. Horsefly stood next to the Toad, her sword drawn and ready, but she had a wide-eyed wariness on her face that did not look at all like her usual confident self. The Toad, still under the ig-troll illusion, stared in horror.

"Pardon me?" Emilina replied, her hands folded primly in front of her. "Are you about to offer more bits of valuable information, Jackal?"

"My name is Natterjack and you...are not Emilina Faust."

Emilina placed her hand on her chest, fingers spread, and made a mocked expression of shock. "Oh my, I'm not the only liar here. I believe in the interest of honesty and truthfulness I should use your real name. You do remember it, don't you?"

Jack looked Emilina straight in the eye. "Of course I do, but its lineage repulses me...Father."

Emilina laughed. It was a resounding, nerve-grating sound as she tossed her head back, continuing to bellow. Her teeth were twisted and gnarled daggers in her mouth. She lowered her gaze to Jack. "I coulda never fool thee for longa, my childah."

Emilina began shaking her head like a wet dog and the movement traveled down her entire body. The bits that looked like Emilina were shed, dissipating into the darkness, leaving only the large, hulking form of Grisswell.

"I can cast illusions as well as thee. It runs in the family." Grisswell's voice growled out the words.

Jack, barely knee-high to the demon, looked up and began to reply. Before he could get the words out, a thundering wall of sound blasted past him over his shoulder, striking Grisswell directly in the chest and face. The force spun him around so he faced the opposite direction. The huge, folded membranous wings rustled as his body began trembling.

A sound came from Grisswell and at first it was so

126

unexpected that Jack didn't recognize it. He was chuckling. "She has grown stronga. Very good!" The demon slowly turned around.

Jack couldn't help but wince when he saw the damage that the blast had wrought. The scaled, leathery skin that covered Grisswell's chest and face had peeled back like old dried paint, exposing the yellow, twisted bone beneath. But even as Jack watched, the flesh began to crawl back over the wounds and knit itself together. A moment later Grisswell stood before him, complete and undamaged.

The demon looked at the imitation ig-troll, bared his teeth in a huge smile, and touched three gnarled black fingers to his cracked lips to blow her a kiss. A small black ball of smoke shot out from between his pursed lips and streaked toward the Toad.

Jack shouted in alarm and leaped toward her, but it was too late. The dark kiss slammed into the already unsteady Toad. Her shot at Grisswell had drained her. The spell struck her, sending both her and the fairy sprawling a distance away. Grisswell's magic blew apart her protective illusion. The fairy leaped to her feet almost immediately but the Toad, who no longer looked like a troll, did not stir.

Jack spun, his large eye beginning to burn with an emerald radiance. "Leave her alone! You can't have her."

Grisswell tossed his head back and laughed his terrible, heartless laugh.

Jack thrust his hands out in front of himself and let loose a tremendous shout. With it the emerald fire that had been born in his eye increased and exploded forth, issuing from his eye, his mouth, and his hands.

The conflagration enveloped Grisswell and some of the writhing clusters of crines near and behind him. The skeletal birds twisted and spasmed in silent agony, then fell into a smoldering, clattering heap on the floor. Grisswell stood unaffected amidst the pile of bones and beaks.

"I knew that it was your magic that felled the Sisters' minions but, Jackal, Jackal...you know that impish fire cannot harm the Keth. There is no need to waste your meager power. I do not seek the Toad...or your newfound friends." Grisswell smiled a wicked smile at Horsefly, Sootfoot, and Pug.

"You lie! You serve the Sisters!" Jack spat at him.

"Indeed we serve those who summon us, but they did not send me hence. I came unbidden to speak witha thee, my son." Grisswell's lips twisted into a smirk when he saw Jack scowl at the word *son*.

"I have nothing to say to you, nothing has changed. Not you, not me," Jack said.

Grisswell looked at the small body of the Toad and said, "Something has changed, and very much."

"I don't need you. I never have. I still reject you and the Keth. Nothing you have to say can..."

"You can save her, Jack," Grisswell interrupted, but his voice had lost some of its menace.

Jack looked at the Toad and back at Grisswell. "What do you think I'm trying to do?"

"The path you have chosen will not bear thee to freedom. Take the Vow, be elevated to your purpose and place. Leave the Kitchen and take her with you. The Sisters will not be able to block your passage."

"No. Even if I could get her out that way, it wouldn't work out for the Toad and you know it." Jack sneered at the looming demon.

"But thee would win thy freedom," Grisswell offered, his hands outstretched in a welcoming gesture.

"That's old bait, and it stinks." Jack began gesturing and murmuring in a strange language but stopped when Grisswell spoke.

"There is no need for a banishment. I have said my piece. I am summoned elsewhere." Grisswell paused. "When next I see thee ... Jackal, you will take your place at my side."

"Father ..." Jack said as the darkness began to spiral around the demon.

"Yes, child." Grisswell cocked his head and smiled.

"Go to hell."

Grisswell laughed again, the sound echoing well after he vanished into a dissipating column of darkness and silence. The quiet lasted only a moment until the crines started clicking and hissing ... and coming closer.

CHAPTER TWENTY

orsefly stood over the Toad, her single blade in her left hand. With her right hand she created a small ring of wavering fairy fire. It wasn't big enough to stretch all the way to Jack and the two Wickers; there were more than a few stone's distance between them after Grisswell's assault. But it was holding the crines back. Though, as they crushed in closer around her, she could feel the ring beginning to weaken. The Toad was alive, at least, but she simply would not wake up. The fairy reached out and slapped the Toad soundly on the thigh with the flat of her blade. Still the Toad did not wake.

Suddenly, a crine leaped high, up and over her fairy fire and landed right in front of Horsefly. The fairy spun, whipping the blade of her sword around in a high arc and severing the bird's head as it stabbed toward the Toad. The crine fell into two pieces but did not die, the body lurching toward the hissing head. In frustration, Horsefly lit fairy fire within its breastbone. The body began to twist and squirm as the bone began to blacken, yet still it lurched toward its skull. Suddenly inspired, Horsefly directed her fairy fire at the unconscious Toad, right on top of the Toad's large webbed foot.

The Toad let loose a high-pitched squeal and leaped to her feet. She stood panting with her hind leg raised like a wounded dog, but something more was wrong. Her eyes were filled with white, pearlescent smoke.

Alarmed, Horsefly jumped to the Toad's side and asked her if she was hurt. The Toad just growled a low menacing rumble and sniffed the air. The fairy waved her hand in front of the Toad's face. There was no reaction. She appeared to be blind.

At that moment the Toad stiffened all over, and suddenly began barking out the ig-troll language. Only this time it was much, much louder and full of force. Everyone present could feel the rumble of the sound through their bones. She snapped out three long, excruciatingly loud whistles, and then collapsed back into unconsciousness in a tumble on the floor. The sounds were so loud and piercing that all of the crines, even the altered ones, jumped back from the circle of fairy fire.

The fairy kneeled next to the Toad and tried to shake her awake again. In the distance she could hear the imp yelling at them. She couldn't understand what he was saying, and, in a moment, it wouldn't matter. The crines were already starting to advance again. The one she had cut down reached its head and the bones grew back together almost as soon as it thrust its spiny neck back into its skull. The fairy crouched and looked all around her. Though she was at least as fast as the trolls, there was no avenue, no direction, that she could use as an escape route. The crines were too close, too packed in together now, and the fairy fire was almost gone. She could cast more but not enough to make a path out of this seething hoard of beak and bone.

In the midst of all this, it was easy to miss the beginning of a low rumbling. By the time anyone noticed, it was too late to be avoided.

From above, it looked like a crashing tidal wave. But this surge wasn't composed of ocean brine and sea foam. It was made of crushing tooth and claw, muscle and sinew, and silent, blind ferocity.

The ig-troll stampede swept up from behind the skeletal birds, their gnashing, slavering, sharp-toothed maws open and snapping at anything that they crossed. There were hundreds of them, perhaps thousands. The first of the trolls slammed into the crines, their talons clicking and swiping at the air as they were bowled over. As soon as they struck the ground the trolls battened their powerful jaws onto legs, ribs, wings and began grinding and ripping fragments of bone away. Those crines that remained

standing found themselves being scaled like a castle wall under siege and it didn't take long for the trolls to take them down as well. Though they seemed to be in a mindless frenzy, the trolls first ripped at the tendons connecting the bone birds' joints, gnawing them apart and collapsing one crine after the other. In moments, the first crines that fell were reduced to small white shards strewn about the floor, their black marble eyes crushed in the jaws of the larger trolls.

From where Natterjack stood it was like watching a slow-moving wave of darkness as the horde of crines began to fall, the army of talon, beak, and bone flattening.

Jack sprang into action, grabbing Pug and Sootfoot roughly around their arms. "Stand close, I've gotta cast another illusion." From behind him, the rumbling footfall and gnashing of troll teeth grew ever closer.

"Are we gonna look like trolls again?" Pug asked as he stepped closer.

"No," Jack said. As he began casting, Pug looked down at himself but nothing was happening. Pug glanced up at Jack, confusion in his eyes. "They can't see us. We need to *smell* like trolls."

Looking past Jack, Pug felt his confusion erupt into fear.

Jack turned as the first troll reached them, a medium-size creature about the size of Pug. It leaped into the air, straight at Natterjack's head. He spun and swatted the creature with an open iron hand, and the troll fell sideways to the ground, clearly stunned. Jack whipped around to Sootfoot. "Now you, quickly!" And he began casting again.

From around his left side a small troll suddenly rocketed into Sootfoot. The impact lifted him off the ground and sent him skidding on the floor. The creature was on him instantly. It opened its slavering jaws and snapped them shut on Sootfoot's shoulder, gripping him like a dog shaking an old rag. Sootfoot screamed.

Jack closed his eye in concentration and finished his spell.

The troll instantly released Sootfoot, but, in one lightning-quick motion, turned and sprang at Jack. Jack took a stumbling step backward and caught the smaller creature in his large hand. As it snapped at his hands and face, drooling with ferocity, Jack turned and threw it as hard as he could. The troll spun wildly in the air, then spread out its forelimbs and small membranous folds of skin that stretched between its arms and sides. The troll stopped spinning and glided roughly to the ground. It hit the floor hard, but as soon as it did, it rolled, turned, and sped straight back at Jack. The troll was immediately joined by three others, the largest of which was as big as Jack. He finished the spell just as the snarling beasts landed in front of him, the largest skidding to a stop. Jack and the creature were nose-to-nose. The troll sniffed twice, turned its head left and right, then all four took off in a different direction toward a stumbling crine. Jack turned to see Pug trying to bandage Sootfoot's shoulder, looking around in a panic.

"Is he okay?" Jack asked.

"Well he'll live if that's what yer askin', but Jack... look..."

Pug pointed at the Toad and fairy, or at least where they had been. The wavering fairy fire was gone. The only thing that remained was a large streak of dark red on the floor.

During the midst of the stampede, Jack had lost sight of the Toad and fairy. The battle moved away from him as he, Pug, and Sootfoot stood back-to-back, cloaked in their magical scents. He glanced over to where the little barrier of fairy fire had been. The fire was gone, as were Horsefly and the unconscious Toad. He motioned to Pug, signaling him to pick up Sootfoot and carry him. Pug began to speak and Jack held up a finger to his lips, silencing him. The trolls couldn't see them or smell them, but Jack didn't want to risk making any noise. It was only because of the noises of nearby fighting that the trio had escaped notice thus far. Jack insisted that they continue on without speaking. The beasts might very well attack the sound of their voice without stopping to check if they were trolls.

Jack pointed in the direction of Guthrie's break.

Natterjack and Pug, with Sootfoot's thin and trembling form cradled in his thick arms, began to slowly and silently thread their way through the carnage and debris of the battle. Luckily, most of the activity had moved farther away, but Jack noticed with more than a little interest that the trolls had left sentinels dispersed throughout the piles and scatterings of crine parts. Each time a piece of bone began to move, as the skeletal birds began to try and rejoin, a guardian ig-troll would hear it, rush over, and crush the shard into smaller pieces in its powerful jaws. Solitary trolls were rapidly darting their way around the room and the air was filled with the sounds of crunching bone. So the beasts could strategize as well as act on instinct. Jack was stunned and impressed.

As they wove their way toward the dish cabinet, Jack noticed that the trolls had not escaped losses in the fight. Because of their sheer numbers and ferocity, they had overwhelmed the crines, but they had suffered as well. Interspersed among the tangled deadfalls of crine skeletons, brown, leathery forms could be seen, broken and unmoving.

It was very slow going, but they finally reached the corner of the china cabinet outside the break. Jack stole a quick look. To his relief, there were no creatures, not even a stray troll, on the other side of the cabinet. The one thing that he did notice and didn't like at all was the long thin trail of blood that led directly toward the soft blue illumination of Ol' Guthrie.

Jack stepped around the cabinet. As he felt the light that marked Guthrie's break touch his face it was as if an electrical charge that had been ever present in his body turned off. His muscles, his shoulders, came unbunched and his back straightened. He sighed a deep calming breath. A moment later, Pug, still carrying Sootfoot, stepped out as well. Sootfoot, though unconscious, stopped trembling almost at once.

Guthrie's break was not large, being only four stone by eight, but it seemed bigger because of the light that permeated the area. Though the cool blue light was dim, the complete absence of shadows made it seem very bright. It was no wonder the fairies had named the place StillBright Hollow.

No creatures hunted here, no one lived here. The break had only one full-time resident.

Ol' Guthrie was the first thing you saw after stepping through the bluish curtain of light. He had been called Ol' Guthrie for as long as anyone could remember, and there were some very old folks in the Kitchen. Compared to normal residents of the Kitchen he was enormous. In fact, he was only a sleeping man.

He was a seemingly normal, wizened old man. Deep wrinkles wove gently across his pale face, and he was dressed in a cream-colored robe, decorated with an intricate light green brocade. One could always find him sleeping soundly in a thick bentwood rocking chair that sat near a small breakfast table, his old arthritic fingers laced together and resting in his lap.

He had been there sleeping for as long as there had been folks in the Kitchen to notice him, which had been hundreds, if not thousands, of years. He had been there so long that he was the most well-known landmark in the Kitchen.

Jack squinted, but as his eye slowly adjusted to the relative brightness he saw a slick streak of blood on the floor that led directly to ig-trolls clustered at Guthrie's feet. His heart sank when he saw that they were all sitting and lying in a wide circle around a bulbous, motionless form at their center.

He leaned over to Pug, who was still blinking rapidly against the light and whispered, "Please tell me it's not the Toad."

Every single pair of troll ears snapped to attention and swiveled toward him. More than one of them peeled their lips back, silently baring their daggerlike teeth.

"Wait here," Jack said and took a cautious step forward. Though no one had ever been attacked in Guthrie's break, there had been a great number of things happening lately that had never happened before, and Jack was prepared to be cautious.

Some of the trolls sat up on their haunches as he drew nearer. They did not appear to be aggressive, just a little wary and curious about him. He took a few more cautious steps forward. He could see a bit better but not by much. What he could see didn't fill him with hope. Whatever was at the center of their circle was covered in thick red blood.

Jack had made his way to within an arm's reach of the nearest troll and, taking a chance, he stretched out his large iron hand. The ig-troll sniffed at him. Jack's scent illusion must have dissipated as they entered the break because the troll made a low growl deep in its muscular chest. It was not being fooled, and this could be trouble.

A dusky grunt issued from the backside of the circle and instantly the growling troll dipped his head and backed away, leaving an opening for Jack.

The small, old troll that the Toad had called Gristle sat next to the small body on the floor: a young ig-troll that had been skewered by a shard of crine beak.

"He died helping the others to protect me," a voice said solemnly. A huddle of larger ig-trolls parted and the Toad stepped into view. "It's the one that I freed from Horsefly's binding; he still has the marks on his wrists and ankles. He answered my call with the rest."

Jack looked at her for a long moment. Inside he was rejoicing and wanted nothing more than to run over and scoop her up with a big hug, but he didn't know how the trolls would react. He saw the pain on her face and he wanted to try his best to console her.

"You saved him and he saved you," Jack said. "You fought so that he could have a chance to live and when you called for help he came, to do the same for you."

"Jack, after your fa...after the demon...did whatever it was that he did...when I woke, it was like I was a troll. I mean, I actually thought I was a troll. I was even blind, as they are. I called for help...and they came. All of them, from everywhere."

"Are you okay? I mean, physically?"

"Yeah," she said simply. "I have a couple of scrapes but that's it."

She seemed so calm. He was impressed by her.

"Where's the fairy?" he asked, glancing around.

"I don't know," she said. "After I called the trolls, I must have passed out again because the next thing I knew I was in here. Gristle was standing over me, but Horsefly...I don't know." She shook her head; her eyes were downcast.

Jack decided to risk a hug after all.

CHAPTER TWENTY-ONE

The ig-trolls left.

The Toad had barked out a few odd clicks and whistles and the creatures simply gathered themselves and their dead companion and silently loped away.

She turned to Jack. "I've asked enough...too much, already."

"But we still have some things to do," Jack replied as Pug plodded up with Sootfoot still cradled in his arms.

"I thought them things was gonna camp out here all day."

Sootfoot was apparently feeling much better, though a little flustered and exhausted. "Will someone please tell Sir Pug that I am perfectly capable of walking? He refuses to put me down. It's my shoulder that's aching, not my foot, for mercy's sake."

"We're all going to have to be on our feet when we leave the break," Jack said. "We'll have to move quickly and we might have some company if any of those crines have reformed."

Pug gently placed Sootfoot on the floor and asked, "So you're really goin' to see the Widows?"

"Yeah," Jack responded. "They're the only ones that might be able to help us find out why the Sisters want her." He pointed an iron finger at the Toad. "And answer where she came from, and what her name is . . . and maybe, how to get her out."

"Might?" said the Toad. "Maybe?"

Jack ignored her concern. "The tricky part is keeping your eye . . . or eyes, in your case, on the path. When we step out of the break we'll be headed in the right direction but we'll only stay that way if we can see our destination. If one of us can keep our eyes on the Widows' Clock at all times then we have a good chance of getting close."

"That doesn't sound very difficult," she said.

"It all depends," Jack responded.

"On what?"

Pug interjected, "On whether or not yer running fer yer lives."

"Exactly," Jack agreed. "And whether or not the path goes wild."

143

"What do you mean, wild?" the Toad asked. "I thought the part of the Kitchen around Guthrie was stable."

"It is on the way in. On the way out, the path can change or move. It can be different each time. Sometimes it's longer, other times it's shorter. Occasionally, as you get close to the clock, the actual landscape transforms. That's when it's especially crucial to keep your eyes on the face of the clock. Otherwise you could find yourself lost again."

"We could get lucky. The path might be still. It sometimes is, at least for a short while, especially for travelers coming from the break," Sootfoot said, attempting a half-hearted smile.

"We?" Jack said.

"We've decided to accompany you for a while, if you'll have us. I mean, it is the only decent thing to do and well, we . . . ah."

"We jus' don't wanna get munched by that damned demon," Pug said, interrupting. "He saw us back there and now he knows us, knows we was helpin' you. We figure we'd be safer with you. All's we have is Sootfoot's flute and that ain't much defense against Grisswell's type."

"You're both in agreement on this? Even though it'll likely be dangerous?" Jack said, eyeing them seriously.

Pug and Sootfoot nodded in unison.

"Then I guess the only question is do we leave now or wait for Horsefly to show up?"

The Toad looked out at the calm of Guthrie's break and

then up at the gentle sleeping face of Guthrie himself. "If she's still alive I think she'll be able to find us. If she's not, then waiting only wastes time."

Jack nodded his head in agreement. "I've never seen anyone, not even another fairy, that can track and hunt like she can. If she's still alive and kicking she'll be back. You made a deal with her. She won't walk away from that."

"Jack..." the Toad began, "why can't we just ask Guthrie the way out of the Kitchen?"

"Others have tried. He always sends them to the front door. No one except the Sisters can get out that way. The door is usually sealed and guarded from the outside."

"Maybe we could wait till it opens, then sneak past the guards. I know it wouldn't be as easy as that, but I'll bet we could figure a way to do it."

Jack was shaking his head. He lowered his eye to meet hers and when he did she could see that he was very serious. "You think others haven't tried that, too? You can't, and I mean *can't*, sneak past Grisswell."

She could understand Jack's reaction. If she ever saw that thing again it would be too soon, and she wasn't related to it.

Sootfoot broke in, "It isn't worth thinking about. Now, the Widows are strange and a bit aloof. But they can be helpful, even if they are a little hard to understand sometimes. *And* they're much closer than the front door is from the break."

"They're our best chance at some solid, reliable information. Even if they can't tell us how to get you out, there's a good shot that they can help you remember something from before. They've done it with others," Jack said.

"How can they get my memory back?" the Toad asked.

"It's hard to explain; it would be easier to show you when we get there."

"Yeah, okay. But after"—she looked hesitant—"will you tell me about...the demon?"

"You can say it, he's my father. And, yeah, I'll tell you everything, but I gotta warn you, it isn't a happy tale." He looked away, but when he looked back at the Toad his eye had recovered its emerald green sparkle. "We'll trade. I'll tell you my past and you can tell me yours."

"There, that oughtta do it," Pug said as he finished redressing Sootfoot's wounded shoulder. He turned to the Toad. "I'll tell ya about my da, too, if ya want. My mum, my granddad, cousins, nephews, nieces. Oh, and my memaw. Now she was an ornery bulldodger. Used to chew guff leather and spit at dingflies."

The Toad sighed, but she was smiling finally, if only a little. "What's guff leather? No, wait, save that for later. I'm too tired to think straight." The Toad turned to Jack. "Do you think we could camp here for a short while? Is it safe enough to sleep?"

"Yeah," Jack said as he pulled a brass watch from one of his pockets and studied it. "I haven't slept in a while and this is the best place to try and get some shut-eye. We all need it. It should be safe enough. Even if they suspect we're here the Witches won't come into the break. Its magic is too peaceful for their wicked sensibilities to take."

They made a small camp under Guthrie's bentwood rocker. The break did appear to be safe as Jack had said but they all had a tough time relaxing enough to rest. The last one to fall asleep was Sootfoot and then only after he had his flute held tight against his chest. None of them slept deeply and their dreams were not comforting.

Some time later, the small group began to stir. They awoke in generally somber moods with equally somber stomachs. They all brightened noticeably when Pug discovered a small patch of what he called "Thistlepops" growing between two stones just under the far leg of Guthrie's table.

"Don't eat 'em outright," Pug said, "or an hour from now you'll give the glue poopers a run fer their coin. Just tuck 'em in yer cheek and suck on 'em fer a while. When they git bitter spit 'em out. It'll knock the edge offa yer hunger till we get some proper food."

"Good find, Pug," Jack said. "This will keep the Toad focused on her question and not on her hunger."

The Toad, rousing herself from her post-sleep grogginess, asked, "What question?"

"You have to ask Guthrie for directions."

"Oh, I thought we all would or you."

"Nope, just you. You're the one with the most to gain," Jack replied.

"What do I do?" she asked as she looked up into Guthrie's old, wizened face.

"Ask for directions," Jack said with a mischievous smile on his face.

She hopped out and squatted, looking up at the sleeping man. "Excuse me, sir, can you please direct me to the Widows' Clock, if you don't mind?"

Ol' Guthrie, who had been sleeping for countless generations, continued to sleep his deep unending sleep. He just sat there doing absolutely nothing. The Toad looked at Jack for guidance.

"Right. It's time to get moving."

The Toad, being the perceptive sort, couldn't help but ask, "Wait. Where are we going? Guthrie didn't answer me."

"He doesn't have to. You ask him the way, keep the question in your mind when you step out of the break, and you find yourself on the right path . . . that's how it works," Jack explained. "Are we ready?"

Jack led them over to the shallow curtain of soft blue light. "When we step out, remember, keep your eyes on the goal but move as fast as you're able. Don't lose sight of the person in front of you or the path may twist, and don't try for any shortcuts—there won't be any. If we get separated, make your way back here and ask Guthrie for directions again."

"That's all there is to it?" the Toad asked.

"An' don't get eaten by nuffin'," Pug said firmly.

However, when they stepped through the curtain of light that defined the edges of Guthrie's break it became obvious, to everyone's relief, that it was unwarranted. There simply weren't any creatures around to eat them. The igtroll herd had left. If the crines had begun to reform they weren't making a show of it. Most of all, the path was entirely clear to the traveling group.

"Wow!" the Toad said, her eyes wide.

It was as if the furnishings of the Kitchen had decided to help them out. Ahead of them, straight as an arrow, the cupboards, cabinets, miscellaneous crates, kegs, and tables were parted. Their path was laid out before them like a cobblestone road and in the distance something glinted in the darkness high above the floor.

"Is that it?" she asked in excitement, amazed at how much farther she could see now. "Is it really that close?"

"It's farther than it looks, but, yeah, that's it," Jack said, grinning, unable to fully contain his own excitement.

They all began to walk, Jack in the lead, at a fast pace. Their excitement was so high they would have sprinted, but he wouldn't let them.

"Don't run unless something's chasing you," he said, smiling.

"Something is always chasing me," the Toad said with a chuckle.

And of course, soon enough, that wouldn't seem so funny.

CHAPTER TWENTY-TWO

That **imp's** a wretched nuisance," Sarafina said as she left the study and continued down the hall toward the stairs that led up to her room. The moment she set her sizeable shoe on the first step she felt someone watching her.

"Grisswell, is that you?" she looked into the shadows surrounding the staircase. There was no answer.

She put her hand on the banister and began to mount the stairs. She glanced up and stopped in midstep. At the top of the stairs a small black eye glinted at her. The misbehaving crib had been lost in the Kitchen with the Toad. How had it gotten out?

"Stay," she ordered, eager to examine it again. The cribs always minded her—well, mostly always. Perhaps she wasn't being commanding enough.

"Stay!" she said as loudly and firmly as she could.

The crib clicked its beak at her twice, then backed away from the edge of the landing and out of sight. Disobedient wretch.

"STAY!" she bellowed loudly and thundered her way up the stairs after the sabotaging bird.

She could hear the click of the crib's clawed feet as it scurried down the dark hallway just off the landing.

Sarafina turned the corner, her breath heaving in her breast, just in time to catch a fleeting glimpse of the bone bird's small, pale foot as it disappeared around the door-jamb to her bedroom.

She smiled. There was no other way out of the room. The smile wavered as she noticed that her door was open. She never, ever left her door open. It was her only modicum of privacy and she never forgot.

She walked over, stepped through the door, and closed it firmly behind her. Immediately the candled sconces on the wall blazed into life, illuminating the room in a dingy, flickering yellow light.

She glanced around, trying to spot the disobedient crib. "Under th' bed," she mumbled to herself. "Must be. Nowhere else for it to go. If it's broken my dollhouse..." Sarafina raised a broad, doughy palm and a candle flew from the wall to her.

Once again she found herself peering into her strange, piecemeal dollhouse. She squinted in the gloomy light of the flickering candle. The crib was not in the dilapidated construction, nor was it under the bed. Just as she turned to scan the room once more she saw a small dim pulse of light radiate up from the nest in the corner of the doll-house. Her brow knitted as she leaned in closer to examine the woven twigs and brambles.

The silver pin that had been so easy to miss before was now plainly visible. It glowed slightly with a dull red throb as if it had been heated in a forge.

Sarafina touched it lightly with the tip of her finger. It wasn't hot at all and the glow instantly faded.

"I see we've made a discovery." Emilina stepped out of a shadow in the corner of the room. The shadow seemed to linger around the Book, pulsing with its own dark power.

Sarafina, in her shock and surprise, almost toppled over onto her mock dollhouse. "What are you doin' in my room?" she demanded.

"Solving a very simple riddle that you have been unable to." Emilina's voice dripped with derision.

Sarafina's hand clenched into a sizeable fist. Emilina, raising a totally unconcerned eyebrow, continued, "I cannot for the life of me understand how you have allowed yourself to be outwitted by a crib. For pity's sake, it doesn't even have a brain...a trait you apparently share. You know that anything that has resided in the Kitchen for very long is altered, sometimes infected by its magic. Your pet crib, the little nuisance, must have stolen a pinfetcher pin and placed it in this nest. It somehow opened a tiny doorway into the Kitchen, to the very nest it was taken from."

Sarafina shuddered with rage, her pale pink cheeks flushed cherry red. She took a menacing step toward Emilina. At least, it would have menaced anyone other than her iron-willed sister.

Emilina stood as still and unshakeable as a spike driven into a stone. She raised her empty hand and in the next instant she was holding the dollhouse as one holds a serving platter: on the tips of her fingers. The dollhouse was a heavy conglomeration of boards but it rested on her hand as if it had no weight at all.

Sarafina sputtered. "You can't have it!" she bellowed.

"I don't want it," Emilina said, almost laughing at her sister. "But I am going to use it for a while and I assure you, it has a better chance of surviving with me than with you."

"You can't..." Sarafina began but Emilina cut her off.

"I will give it back. Sister...I have allowed you to keep it thus far, haven't I? You mustn't believe that it was hidden from me. I could have made you remove it long ago but I am kind, am I not? Now, go fetch me a few leaves from the bush that grows by the gate in front of the house and meet me back in the study in one quarter of an hour."

Sarafina wilted as she always did. She turned and began to trudge out of her room, unconsciously pausing by the door to wait for Emilina's inevitable parting blow.

"And don't stop to peck at any seeds along the way."

CHAPTER TWENTY-THREE

**hey were making** excellent progress, though Jack had been right; the clock was much farther than they thought when they first exited the break. The quartet had been walking for quite some time but only seemed fractionally closer to their objective. The Toad had just opened her mouth to chat when a horrible screeching sound began in the distance.

They stopped dead in their tracks. It was coming from behind them and increasing quickly in volume, but before she could turn to look, Jack grabbed her head and held it forward.

"Don't look, keep your eyes on the clock. Got it? One of us has to, and I'm betting that Pug and Sootfoot have already turned around. Am I right, boys?"

"J-Jack, y-you hafta see this!" Pug stuttered, panicked.

"Yeah, but..." the Toad started, but Jack broke in.

"I'll keep my hand on you while I look back, okay? Keep moving forward, slowly. We don't want to lose Pug and Sootfoot, but the path may twist at any moment."

She did as he asked but the second that he turned he gripped her tighter. In that same moment she felt the very stones beneath her feet rise up and fall like an ocean surge, carrying her with them.

The next instant, she was scooped up in Jack's large iron hands and cradled to his chest as he sprinted along the path at a breakneck speed.

Suddenly terribly afraid at what might make Jack act so alarmed, she only barely managed to keep her eyes glued to the glinting surface in the far distance. She yelled at Jack, "What is it? What's going on?"

"The path. It's closing behind us. Too fast!" He had to shout in order to be heard over the tremendous wind that had just blasted up from behind them.

"Jack, are you looking at the clock? Let me look!" she shouted.

"Okay, but be quick!"

She risked a glance back over her shoulder—intending to only look for a second—but what she saw chilled her blood and she couldn't turn away from the sight.

He was right, the path was closing, but it wasn't just that. The Kitchen was seething. It was like suddenly finding oneself at the edge of a stormy sea. The cabinets, crates, and tables that had so distinctly lined their way now slammed together with terrible force. Pieces were splintering and breaking and other smaller bits of furniture were crushed entirely. Pots, pans, and other utensils were flung everywhere. And the tide was catching up to them.

Pug and Sootfoot were only a half stone behind them. Sootfoot was jack-legged and built for running but Pug wasn't, and he was having a dangerously hard time keeping up.

She turned back toward the clock and saw to her dismay that the churning of the Kitchen had begun to spread past them like a ripple traveling out over the water. The surge that she had felt through the floor only moments ago was happening again and again, with increasing severity, forcing the companions to race over them, up and down and up and down.

"Jack! You have to put me down and pick up Pug!" she shouted over the smashing of wood and the increasing roar of the tumultuous Kitchen.

"No! You can't keep up!" he replied.

"I'm faster than he is. If you don't, he'll be crushed!" And with that, she did what many toads have done to their unwitting grabbers throughout time: She suddenly squirmed and kicked, flinging herself out ahead at the undulating path.

Jack shouted something at her that was mostly lost in the increasing noise but she was pretty sure that she wouldn't have wanted to hear it if she could. Impish swearwords were shockingly descriptive.

Jack dropped back for the instant that it took for Pug and Sootfoot to catch up to him. As they passed him he lunged and swept Pug up, holding him securely under his right arm. Sootfoot was moving fast and as Jack resumed his full-ahead tilt they were scrambling side-by-side. He kept his eye on the Toad. She was doing an excellent job of keeping her eyes on the clock face. It was getting closer, but still seemed much too far away.

She was right, she was much faster than Pug; in fact, her leaps were only becoming longer and longer. As Jack watched her, his sharp eye picked out the reason instantly: She had grown a thin leathery membrane between her arms and sides. She was traveling in the quick hopping glide of an ig-troll.

She doesn't even know she's doing it, Jack thought to himself as he watched her jump and cling sideways to a large keg. *She's going to outpace us if she doesn't slow down.*

The Toad leaped and sprang, again and again, until she was just a small green blur in the distance.

Jack slowed his speed just enough to let Sootfoot get a single stride ahead of him. In an effort to try to slow the crushing walls of furniture closing in on him from behind, he reached out with his left hand and swiped at a small wooden pedestal. It fell and a moment later he heard the closing path pulverize the obstacle, but it didn't seem to slow its gnashing progress for more than an instant. As he ran, he continued to pull whatever bits of tables and chairs he could manage into the maw of the Kitchen. It was still much too close behind him.

The Toad stopped; she had arrived and stood about five stone from the base of the tower at the edge of a large octagonal patch of blue-green grass. In the distance, at its center, loomed the clock—a grandfather clock, but it was huge, much larger than any normal clock would have been . . . and it was not unguarded.

The chaotic crushing path behind Jack seemed to realize that he was escaping and its rending, smashing cacophony intensified. Jack, Pug, and Sootfoot were only a few stone from the Toad when the floor lurched sideways and a low, three-legged stool leaped in front of them, sending them sprawling. Jack jumped to his feet and circled his arms tightly around the two Wickerfolk. He saw the sides of the path begin to shudder around them. The opening to the Widows' Clock slammed shut just as he launched himself through to the clearing where the Toad now stood.

Where there would have been the sound of crushing bone and crumpling iron, there was only the fading echo of cracking, impacting wood. The wind and the roar of the Kitchen ceased, as did the surging chaos of movement, the moment that they had leaped from the path onto the grassy clearing.

Jack raised himself up on his elbows, gasping for breath. He looked at the Toad, whose ig-wings had disappeared. She looked as normal as she always had. She was staring up at the clock, her mouth hanging open in utter disbelief.

"Jack," she said evenly, not at all out of breath like someone who had just been hopping or gliding for her life, "you never said how big..." Her gaze slowly rose from the bottom of the clock tower to the top, far above her. Her eyes rested on the gold-trimmed clock face, and it was so high that she was nearly falling over backward with the effort.

"It appears that the Widows employ a contingent of sentries. Will they pose a problem?" Sootfoot was the first to recover his wind.

They had all recently faced a hoard of despicable crines and a herd of ferocious ig-trolls, but as Jack's eye followed Sootfoot's he felt the tingle of gooseflesh ripple across his body.

"What? Them? How dangerous could a bunch of gigantic, venomous spiders really be?"

CHAPTER TWENTY-FOUR

The clock tower stretched far above the diminutive party. Its surface undulated with hundreds of spiders, and in places it was completely obscured by thickly woven webs. Except for a dim fluttering glow that wavered, as if a small candle had been lit somewhere inside it, the face of the clock was plain.

The Toad noticed with some degree of alarm that a knot of large spiders was forming at the broad black base of the tower. Out of habit, she looked around to find an avenue of escape, but the path behind them had closed, and the grassy lawn was surrounded by the backs of cabinets and chairs. There was nothing to do but wait as three of the largest spiders separated themselves from the rest of the cluster and slowly advanced upon them.

Natterjack smiled nervously. "Relax. There's three of

them, and four of us. We got 'em outnumbered, if their friends don't jump in. They don't really look like jumpers, though . . . they look like biters."

"Not funny," the Toad said. "Any plans?"

Sootfoot interjected, "Might I suggest an immediate retreat? I don't want to be a naysayer but I feel I must point out that each of the trio coming toward us is easily twice as large as you, Jack, and I for one have seen enough of the clock tower. May we please go?"

Pug sputtered, "Izzit always lousy wif spiders or did someone import 'em special fer us?"

"Just hold on, and calm down. First of all, there's nowhere to run. Secondly, we didn't just go through all this to turn tail from a bunch of spiders. There are always spiders at the clock. Just not usually this many."

Jack stepped forward, held up his hands ceremoniously, and began speaking to the spiders. "Oh, great Spiders of the Clock, we come to speak to the Widows. Will you let us pass?"

The largest spider stepped forward and in a nasal, officious voice replied, "Only one may pass. Three must remain and one must be offered as a sacrifice to feed my legion. We will take the fat one."

"What? Which one? The Toad, or the Wicker? 'Cause if it's the Toad, no deal."

Pug began sputtering incoherently in protest.

"Yeah, okay. We'll take the Wicker," the spider agreed, and turned toward Pug.

Pug fainted.

The Toad and Sootfoot caught him and prepared to defend Pug. They both stopped in midstep, listening as a very odd sound erupted from the three spiders. For a moment, neither of the two could recognize it. Jack knew what it was because he was doing it, too.

"You're laughing!?!"

"It wasn't cruel. It was funny," Jack said. "Hold on for a moment and grow a sense of humor, okay?"

"How could you do that to poor Pug? Look at him... he's a wreck," the Toad admonished, pointing at a very pale Pug recovering from his shock.

"He's strung a bit too tight, is all. It's good for him."

"Yeah, well, telling someone who just escaped being eaten by one thing that they're about to be eaten by another is maybe just a little *poor* timing for a joke."

"Mischievous humor is my birthright as an imp." Jack raised his eyebrow in mock indignation.

Another voice cut in: " 'Scuse me, miss, we didn't mean no harm. Me an' my mates here jes' get bored standing

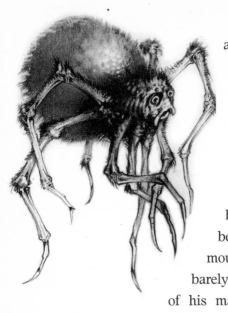

around the clock tower all day and when I saw my friend Jack here makin' such a show of it, I couldn't help meself."

The Toad turned and found herself looking up into eight eyes. Somehow all eight managed to look a bit sheepish even though they belonged to one simply enormous shiny black spider. She was barely as tall as the first joint on one of his many legs. The spider lowered himself, nearly resting on the floor, his knees sticking up in the air. If she was afraid she certainly wasn't showing it. After all, facing down a spider, even one as large as this, seemed a small thing in comparison to her recent journey.

"What was your name again?" she asked.

"M' name? It's Chuck, miss," the spider replied, shifting on his many legs like a caught, guilty child.

"Chuck, don't apologize to me. Apologize to him." She pointed at Pug.

"I've done tried, miss. But he won't have none of it. Will ya tell 'im for us? I mean it was kinda funny, but we all feel bad that he's takin' it so tough. We all din't figure on him havin' a fear of aights."

"A fear of heights?" the Toad asked, confused. "What would that have to do with any . . ."

"No, miss, not 'ights . . . aights. You know . . . aight eyes, aight legs . . . aights."

"Oh!" she said, suddenly getting it. "Eights!" She smiled. "Not so much a 'fear of eights' as a fear of being eaten, which is something I share with him."

"Right. Well anyway, miss, let 'im know, none of us plan on puttin' the bite on 'im, will ya?" The spider made a bow to her and ambled a short distance away.

She turned to give Jack another disapproving stare but he had already walked over to speak to Pug and Sootfoot. She hopped over to them as Pug was getting to his feet.

He shook Jack's outstretched hand. "No harm done, Jack. I like a good gag as well as the next 'un."

"All right, I think it's time to do what we came here to do." Jack looked at the Toad. "Are you ready?"

"Oh, we're being serious now, are we? Yes. I'm ready."

They took off toward the base of the clock tower, Chuck leading the way and escorted on both sides by the other two spiders.

Jack turned to the giant sentry. "Chuck, what brought the legion to the Widows' Clock?"

"Don't really know. We ain't been here long. We were called suddenly from our march by Charnum point—that big burned-out place over by the front door, where Burnard thumps around."

Jack grimaced. "Burnard! Are you guys crazy?" He explained to the Toad, "Burnard is a very ill-tempered pot-bellied stove. Believe me, you do not want to meet him."

"Yeah, he's a foul one at that," Chuck continued. "Anyway, that's where we were when we got summoned by the White Widow. She din't seem in the best of moods but it's hard to tell with that one. You really going to send the Toad in to petition a meetin' with her?"

"What do you mean, 'send the Toad in'? Aren't we all going in?" the Toad jumped in.

"Nope, sorry. That bit before about only one of you gettin' in . . . that part's for real."

"Jack, did you know this?" The Toad stopped walking.

"I know she's seen groups of people before. Is this new?" Jack looked up at Chuck.

"Well, the White Widow ordered it, when we were summoned three days ago as the tower measures time."

Jack's brow furrowed in thought as he fished his watch out of his pocket. "I set my chronometer by tower time and that's when all this mess with the Toad started."

"She said something big was happening in the Kitchen and to only let in one petitioner at a time."

Jack turned back to the Toad. "You still want to go through with it?"

"Oh, sure! Not that I know what I have to do, or even whether or not it's potentially dangerous . . . sure! Why not?"

"Everything is potentially dangerous," Sootfoot said from behind her.

"But I mean really dangerous. You were joking around before because you were worried, right?"

Natterjack shrugged. "I get worried . . . sometimes I make jokes. Other times I explode in a ball of green flames."

"Is it any more dangerous than what we've already been through with the crines and the path? Just tell me there's a good chance that I will be okay." Her eyes were steady and sincere. "If you tell me that . . . I can do it."

"Some people don't make it out. The selfish, the untrue, the unworthy. I think you have a better chance than any-one of getting in and out of the Widows' Clock. The White Widow has a way of knowing things. She's the one you have to see. As for what to expect . . . I've visited the Wid-ows three times in my life and it was different each time. Have no expectations and make no assumptions."

The Toad took a deep breath, closed her eyes, and exhaled. She opened her eyes, turned, and in three quick hops she was standing in front of an intricately etched brass plate hung by a single screw on the huge rectangular base of the clock. Chuck stretched out one long, shiny leg and swung the plate aside, revealing a tunnel of darkness that her night sight could not penetrate.

"No time like the present," she said, not speaking to anyone in particular. "Get it? I'm going into a clock." She chuckled nervously and went in without even a backward glance.

CHAPTER TWENTY-FIVE

ell...here I am...the Toad thought as she crept deeper into the blinding darkness.

But it wasn't just dark in here; it was quiet. A deeper, more complete silence than she had ever known.

"Hello?" It was barely more than a whisper but in the perfect stillness, she winced at how loud her voice had sounded. "Is anyone there?"

She was answered almost instantly and though the voice was low, soft, and silky she nearly jumped out of her skin. "No one is here. We are all here."

The Toad didn't like riddles. "I need to speak to the Widow. Is she here?" She turned around blindly.

The other voice seemed to come from all around her.

"There are many Widows in the clock."

She remembered Chuck's words. "I would like to petition the White Widow."

"The White is but one."

"Can I meet with her?"

"Yes," the voice answered. "But you must agree to The Ordeal of Seven."

"What's that?" she asked.

"The Ordeal of Seven questions. It is passage and payment."

"I probably have more than seven questions, but I'll take it," she replied.

"No," the voice said evenly. "You may ask only one."

"Wait, I don't understand. I thought you said seven?"

The voice replied, "You must answer three questions to speak with the White. You must answer three questions to leave. You may ask one question."

"W-what? One . . . one question?" Rage bubbled up within her. Had she fought through so much, had those that fought with her and died, done so for so little?

"I hate this Kitchen! Nothing ever makes sense, nothing is ever *fair*. Fight this . . . fight that . . . go here . . . go there . . . here, let me eat you . . . and if you're supposed to be the good guys, why can't you at least get a damn candle in here . . . a lamp . . . somethin'?"

The smooth voice was nonplussed by her outburst. "Seven questions."

"Fine! Seven questions, let's get on with it!"

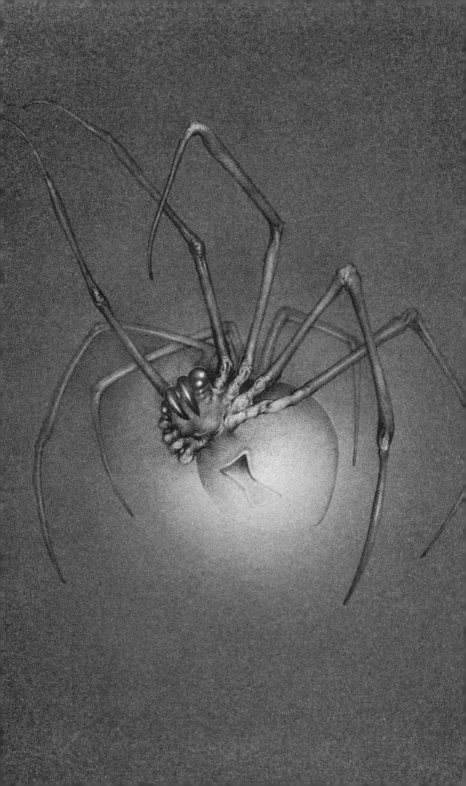

She stood there and the only sound she could hear was her own enraged exhalations. After a few moments she began to breathe more regularly. The fire of her anger slowly diminished. "Can we please get on with it?" she asked.

At that moment she noticed the darkness was changing. A dim red glow had begun to grow from off to her right somewhere. The radiance increased and she could see something moving toward her. As it came closer, the radiance brightened and she could just make out what it was.

Bloodred in color, the spider crept closer. She was small compared to those outside, but still slightly larger than the Toad. The Toad stepped back, but paused when the enigmatic voice returned. "Be still."

"Are you a Widow?" the Toad asked. "That wasn't my question, was it?"

"You have asked me two questions and neither matter. Only NoNe may answer the One question," she said in her silky, soothing manner. But the spider raised itself on its back legs and the Toad saw an hourglass shape glowing against the slick red carapace of her underbelly.

"I will take you farther. Give me your hand." The spider offered an elongated foreleg and the Toad placed her webbed hand on it lightly. It pulsed with a warm energy.

"Why are you here?" the spider asked.

"Do you mean here in the clock, or here in the Kitchen?" she asked. "I'm in the clock because I need to know why I'm in the Kitchen. That's why I ca..."

But her answer was cut short as the spider sank her venomous fangs into the Toad's green-pebbled forearm. The Toad shrieked once, but the Widow's venom worked very quickly and as she slid to the floor, rapidly losing consciousness, she mumbled, "Hate the...Kitchen."

The Toad's mind slipped into a dream almost at once.

It was a warm, sunlit day. The air was absolutely full of the fragrance of summer, and the trees rustled. The Toad found herself sitting on a small stone that jutted out of a pristine pond watching two humans—a girl, swimming, and a woman on the banks.

"Miss!" the woman called out sternly.

A pair of sky blue eyes turned toward her from the water. "Almost done, Mirabella, just one more dive."

No, not Mirabella...Emilina, the Toad thought. *And the girl...I know her.*

The woman who was not really Mirabella looked down at the girl, shaking her head in refusal.

"No more time, miss. Your father has asked to see you today and if we don't leave now we will miss the opportunity. You do want me to speak with him about your charm, do you not?"

"You know I do. You'd do that? I think Father would listen to you."

"We shall have to see, but there will be no chance of that if we don't meet him before he departs."

"I'm ready, let's go!" she said as she struggled to pull

her dress over the soaking garments beneath. "I hope he agrees with you, Mirabella. I feel so ready."

"You've shown promise, and it has happened before that one of your age and your house has reached First Form early."

"Really? Who was it? I wonder why Father hadn't told me about it."

"I believe your father's second cousin reached First Form and flew as a pelican on his thirteenth, but he was an exceptional child."

"Might as well have been a toad. Who would pick a pelican as their First?" She paused. "And besides, I'm already on my fourteenth."

There was only the slightest hint of indignation in her voice but Mirabella still caught it. "I wouldn't approach your father with that attitude. You know very well that the parents choose the form."

The girl looked at her governess expectantly. "You've seen my charm. If you tell me what it is at least I'll be able to put it out of my head."

"Doubtful." Mirabella cocked an eyebrow at her. "But, if I were to look into the sky one day..."

"Yes..." the girl prodded.

"If I were to look into the sky one day and see a beautiful grey-tipped falcon, it wouldn't surprise me to know its name."

At that moment, if she hadn't been soaking wet, she might literally have burst into flames from excitement. As it was, she began to radiate so much heat that steam rose off her in small wisps.

Mirabella sighed. "Calm yourself, miss, or it's back into the pool and we'll surely be too late for your father."

"I can feel the energy building. Father has to give me the charm soon or I'll change without it."

The woman stiffened at her words. "You cannot! Must not! Without the power it contains you might lose yourself in a host of forms, or worse, become formless. Unless you'd rather be an unthinking puddle of flesh."

"Mirabella, I know that. I was just joking," she said, rolling her eyes and shaking her head.

"Nevertheless, say something like that in front of your father and you will never even see the box it comes in, much less your First Form charm."

"My last governess had a better sense of humor," she replied with a playful smile.

"Indeed. Ask yourself why she is your governess no longer. Now, get in the carriage or we will be last in line to see your father. His council is tomorrow and after that he will be traveling the borders with Prince Orwell. You may not have many opportunities to speak with him after today—at least for a while."

The girl wrung runnels of water out of her hair and then hopped into the open door of the small horse-drawn transport. She was still slightly damp as she slid to the other side of the carriage seat to make room as Mirabella climbed in and sat down.

The Toad suddenly found herself sitting in the seat opposite the two women.

"Why have you not dried yourself? You're going to ruin your dress." The girl was already looking out the opposite window, lost in thought. She must have heard Mirabella after all, though, because a small shimmer floated from the top of her head to the tips of her toes. An instant later she was completely dry, her hair spilling across her shoulders as if it had been coifed that very morning.

The girl was tall for fourteen and poised. She was possessed of hair the color of burnished copper that framed a wide-eyed face that was honest and pretty in that straightforward sort of way. She was slim, because of her height, but not gangly like some.

Mirabella smirked as she noticed the light brown scorch marks at the edges of her dress as the small, black bell carriage began to bump into motion. "Such a talented young lady, your power seems almost unconscious," the governess said. "But so mercurial, and you can never control yourself when you're emotional. Not to mention, you're quite oblivious."

Almost as if to prove the point, the girl wasn't listening.

Jack sat on a large boulder only a few stone away from the base of the clock. The Toad had been gone for hours, and he was bored. "At least she has something to do,"

Jack grumbled to himself. Sootfoot sat cross-legged on the ground busying himself with silent practice on his spiralsong flute. Even Pug was occupied. He had eventually warmed up to the conviviality of the Spider Legion after a few sentries had brought him some dried meat strips and a leather drinking skin of barkwater. He was sitting in a half circle with Chuck and a few others playing Sticks and Stones. It was a name-calling game of the most vulgar sort and while Jack, being an imp, was a very formidable name caller, his worry over the Toad made a poor sportsman of him.

Just then Jack spied something that he hadn't noticed before. A rock, lying on the ground at his feet. He picked it up and gave it a light toss in the air. It smacked against his palm with a solid clang.

"It's too small," he whispered. He started to give it a good fling but, like many artistic types both before and after his time, he noticed something in this humble piece of stone that captured his attention. Perhaps it was an odd jutting angle or a pattern of minerals or maybe it was just the feeling that there was something to be found in the raw material. Whatever the case, there was certainly something special in this stone. And that something had spoken to the part of Jack that could recognize such things. Recognize and reveal. He reached into his pocket and pulled out a leather-wrapped collection of miniature tools. These tools had been made for Jack and as he passed his hand over them and made a gesture of magic, they enlarged to fit his huge hands. He began working, slowly, thoughtfully. As time wore on, something began to emerge.

The Toad woke suddenly, moving from unconsciousness in a snap. She struggled but she couldn't move; in fact, she strained to breathe. Her entire body, save her head, was covered in a banded spiderweb that was strong as iron and reminded her of the fairy braid. When she stopped moving, she also realized that she was swaying, dangling from a thread in midair. She could see a dim greenish glow all around her, and the whole world, or at least the very small part that she could see at the moment, was made of gears. Large, small, silver, brass, iron. They were all turning and the constant grind and click was deafening.

Her arm throbbed intensely where the Red Widow had bitten her. "I guess Jack was wrong," she muttered. "I guess I won't be one of the few who make it out of here. Well, at least I'm not upside down."

"I am," a voice from above her said. "But I'm used to it."

The Green Widow descended from the darkness. She was the smallest spider that the Toad had encountered so far, about the same size as Pug's head. She was incredibly beautiful. Her carapace wasn't just green but had traces of shimmering opalescence racing across its surface. The hourglass on the Widow's belly shifted with a shade of greenish fire that reminded her of Jack.

"Are you going to bite me, too?" the Toad asked. "I've already failed the first question. I mean, if I don't get to go on, what's the point?"

"No one said that you had to answer the questions correctly to proceed, dear, and no one said that you failed," the spider said, her voice as smooth as the other, but with a friendlier tone. "We must ask and you must answer." She paused. "And yes, I will most certainly bite you."

"But why?" she pleaded.

The Green Widow laughed, but she did not answer.

"Fine, but you'd better ask your question soon. I'll probably pass out again!"

"Where do you come from?" the Green Widow asked pleasantly, as she came closer.

In frustration, the Toad barked out, "From my mother! From my father! From a past that I can't remember!"

The spider reached out and clung to the Toad's shoulder, eight jet-black eyes staring. "That was a very good answer, dear."

The Toad screamed as the spider bit into her cheek. The scream was short-lived as her thoughts faded and she found herself dreaming once again.

The small bird pecked at the crushed breadcrumbs in the girl's outstretched palm. She was supposed to wait in the receiving hall until Mirabella called her, but the governess had been in her father's office for hours. Well, a quarter hour at least and that was nearly as long if you're sitting on a hard bench in a receiving room. No, the animal merchant next door was much more diverting than any moldy book.

The Toad sat in a small silver cage in the storefront, once again an invisible observer, but this time she had gone deeper into the dream, and deeper into the girl. She could hear her thoughts as if the girl were speaking them aloud.

Reaching up a finger, the girl ruffled the little bird's head feathers. It chirped at her and began busying itself by smoothing them back down.

"Bibbett," she said softly. Though this bird didn't have a name, birds always made her think of Bibbett. He was a pet kestral she had had when she was young. She cried for days when, after her fourth birthday, she was made to give him up.

"Be free, Bibbett, free forever." She had set the bird free herself, and he had taken a tiny piece of her four-year-old heart with him. As Bibbett leaped into the sky, chirping as it went, she had seen a small blue spark jump from her hand to his chest. As a child, she imagined his chirping said, "I am free!"

She was as comfortable with animals as she was with people, but that wasn't unusual. Her family had always possessed abilities with animals and communication . . . as well as magic. For this reason, they had also always been advisors and attachés, for they were able to understand almost any language. And the magic was politically

179

valuable, too. It was common enough in her family to be able to call upon the shallow rivulets of power, but much less common to be a shape changer as she would be... as her father was. In the entire, ever-expanding kingdom, there were only a handful of families that possessed the magical magnitude required to change physical shape.

This ability, called First Form, was the primary reason that the girl had been denied pets after her fourth birthday. In fact, it was only after her talents had begun manifesting around her tenth that she was allowed even brief proximity to an animal of any sort. A potential shape changer ran the risk of developing their talents early, sometimes imprinting whatever animal happened to be nearby. If they didn't possess a strong self-image, if they didn't have a clear idea of who they were, they could become lost. "Formless," as Mirabella put it, and they would never be human again. The charm her father was going to give her was a totem. It represented an animal that would be the shape changer's "First Form." When the user assumed the shape of the animal, the charm would assume the shape of the human, in miniature, giving the user an image of themselves to focus upon while training, and vice versa. Later, after many years of experience and study, the charm wouldn't be needed anymore.

The girl remembered the explanation that her previous governess, Byjorna, had given when she asked about Second Form. "Nothing to worry about there," the jovial woman had said. "First Form is powerful and draws from the Deep Magic, allowing the wielder to assume the shape of their chosen animal. But where First Form is like drinking a cup of water, Second Form is like being thrown into the well, and much more dangerous to practice. It's hard enough to keep track of one extra shape. Imagine how hard it would be if you could be anything. Hasn't been a Second Form in ten generations. I reckon in ten more, First Form will be lost as well."

That had made her very sad. She hadn't even experienced shape shifting yet and already she felt its loss looming. Certainly not in her lifetime, but someday...

The bird pecked at her hand, startling her out of her thoughts.

How long have I been standing here? She hurried back to the stairs leading up to her father's office. His double doors, bearing a brass plate reading EXTERIUM ADVISOR were still closed. She leaned close and put an ear against the smooth polished wood, holding her breath. She could hear two muffled voices. She exhaled in relief and seated herself on the waiting bench, straightening her dress as she did.

The Toad found herself sitting next to the girl. All of this was so strange and yet...had she dreamed this before? It seemed so.

The door opened and Mirabella called to her, "Come in, miss."

Jack turned the object in his hand. It wasn't finely crafted. The stone had been too small for him to easily handle, but it was...familiar. When he had shown it to Pug and Sootfoot they had both had the same reaction, even though they all agreed that they had never seen anything quite like it before.

As Jack contemplated this, he heard the *Whump!* of something striking the ground behind him. Turning, he saw a small, black marble eye over a very sharp beak.

Click...click, click.

The Toad shivered herself awake, though she wasn't cold at all. Her entire body ached and she was hot with fever. Her cheek had swollen so much that she could barely see out of that eye.

She was still tightly bound but now she was being dragged on a cold hard floor. Turning her head so that she could see out of her good eye, she saw a large black sentinel spider pulling her steadily along the wooden surface.

"Where are...y-you...t-taking...me?" she asked as a shudder racked through her.

A thick, guttural, almost unintelligible voice said, "Sssilver."

The Toad closed her eyes as her head began to swim and when she opened them again she had stopped moving. She lay there, on her back, so weak...tired...She saw movement out of the corner of her eye but she was so... so worn that she didn't care enough to turn and look. One eye was now swollen completely shut.

This is how Jack always sees the world, she thought hazily.

She felt a weight suddenly land on her belly. It slowly made its way up and paused on her chest bone. The Toad knew what it was.

A thin, reedy voice filled her hearing. "I am the Silver. This is your final station. I am obliged to make you aware that you are quite probably dying. If so, your journey ends forever, the Sisters will be victorious, and all those you know will fall. Having duly informed you of the generalities of your potential demise, I hereby ask my question: With the powers at your disposal... why have you not freed yourself from the Red Widows' binding and attempted to escape the clock?"

The Toad's fever-baked brow furrowed. "Because..." she began, bracing herself for the bite that must follow the answer. "I'm tired of running and I'm tired of being afraid."

The Silver crept up to her throat and spoke in a softer tone, almost a whisper. "I judge your answer to be true, and your character to be exemplary."

And as she bit her, the Toad replied, "Great... bury me someplace nice."

Once again the Toad entered the dream but this time she did not seem to be herself at all. She stood...

...and entered her father's office. Where the hall had been utilitarian and impersonal, this room was warm and inviting, all oaks, cherries, and ripple woods. Mirabella stood off to one side and her father sat at his expansive desk. He looked up at her, face brightening with a smile and improving his already handsome bearing.

"Mirabella, give us some time please and if you don't mind, bring us some tea, and some for yourself as well." He said, "I hear someone's been bothersome about an upcoming event and we need to talk about it."

He stood as the governess left the room, walked around the desk, and gave his daughter a huge hug.

"I'm sorry," he said.

"For what?" the Toad found herself replying.

"I'm sorry that I have to leave so soon after returning. We've hardly had any time together and tomorrow I'll be busy in council all day."

She smiled and kissed him on the cheek. "That's okay. I know how you can make it up to me."

From an early age she had understood her father's responsibilities and that his service took him far abroad. When she was younger it had been painful and she wept at his every departure. Though her daily care had been delegated to a long line of "Mirabellas," "Byjornas," and others, her father had raised her after her mother was killed in a horseback riding accident when she was still a baby.

"You're not wasting any time today, are you?" He stood there with an expectant grin beaming on his face.

"What?" She looked at him quizzically. That's when she noticed the small wooden box on the desk that hadn't been there before.

"Is it...?" she started to ask.

"It is, but," he began, "if I give you your First Form charm, you must promise me three things."

"I promise," she said without waiting to hear what his requirements actually were. She reached for the box.

"Hold on." He stepped in front of her. "This is important."

She looked at him and saw that he was serious now, and he wasn't smiling anymore.

"One, you begin your language studies. It won't take you long to get the hang of it, but some dialects are very complicated; you will have to work at it. Two, you approach your disciplines with more focus...more control. Practice every day and night if you have to"—he paused, girding himself for the inevitable outburst his next stipulation would bring—"and three, you cannot assume First Form until I return."

"What? Why? Father, I'm almost ready now, I can feel it," she said.

"I know you are. It's just..." He paused, looking away.

"What?" she asked.

"I just don't want to miss it." He looked back at her. "I want to see you take flight. I want to be there with you...

185

for you..." He embraced her again. "I've missed so much. I don't want to miss this."

"I'll wait," she said. "I do want you to be there. I'm sorry, too, I was only thinking about myself."

He picked up the box and silenced her with a kiss on her forehead. He placed it in her hands. She looked at him and he nodded his permission. She slowly lifted the hinged lid.

"It *is* a falcon! Oh, it's the most beautiful thing I've ever seen!" And it was.

She threw her arms around his neck, almost knocking him over in the process.

She lifted the thin silver chain out of the box. At the end of it was a gleaming representation of a saker falcon, wings folded in the posture of a dive, perfectly detailed down to the striations on its feathers.

He reached out and unclasped the chain. She turned and lifted her hair so that he could rejoin it around her neck.

"It tingles," she said, laughing.

Her father smiled. He had never seen her so happy. "It will for a long while. It's gathering an impression of you. It takes a bit of time for the charm to fill."

"In ancient times they used real animal bones and sometimes the animal itself. It was more powerful," Mirabella said as she entered the room. The tea service rattled slightly as she placed it on a small round table.

"I prefer the silver version, thank you," the girl said, unable to tear her eyes away from the glinting falcon.

"It's true," her father said, "those were harsh times. Either way, the icon isn't nearly as impressive as the animal it represents."

Mirabella began serving the tea. "There's Binberry honey if anyone would like." They both nodded approval.

"I do wish I had been in the room when you opened the box," she said, after serving them. "Though as it was, I heard you all the way down the hall."

She replaced the kettle on the service and smiled at them both. "I see the discussion went well. What a beautiful charm!"

"This tea is too sweet," the girl said as she drank half her cup.

"It really is," her father said, frowning into his own nearly empty cup. "How much Binberry did you use, Mirabella?"

"Only enough to hide the taste of the poison, sir," she said, still smiling.

"W-what did you say?" he said as his hand began to shake and his cup crashed to the floor.

"Yes, sir," she said, at complete ease. "An incredibly quick poison. One drop to paralyze. Three to ... well, make it permanent, shall we say."

The man's eyes glazed over and he followed his cup to the floor.

The young girl's mouth fell wide in surprise as her eyes dulled. Her cup was in her hand, and she was still as stone, still as death, unable to move.

Mirabella snatched the chain from the girl's neck. She coiled it in her hand, falcon sitting in the nest of her palm. She spoke a strange word and gestured over it. It sent a brilliant spark into the air. What had once been the finest silver was nothing but a small pile of dust that she shook from her hand.

"Falcons are so hard to manage." Mirabella walked over and pulled a small red bag from her traveling clutch. She passed her hand over the bag, her fingers twisting into a magical gesture. The bag rapidly doubled and tripled in size. It kept growing until it was exactly big enough to hold a young girl. Mirabella reached into the bag and pulled something out. It struggled in her hands.

"You, wretched girl, are closer to First Form than you know. In twenty-four hours you will change whether you want to or not. The poison that I administered will ensure that. If I left you now, you would most surely be formless, but I am not so cruel. This will be your companion for the time being, until the change is complete." Mirabella held the small wriggling form up to the girl's eyes. Though she could see and feel and hear, she couldn't so much as twitch an eyelid.

The governess tossed the creature into the large red sack.

"Your turn," Mirabella crooned.

She saw the bloodred velvet lining of the sack as it was pulled over her head and the last thing she heard before the poison finally carried her to unconsciousness was a loud and resounding "*CROOOOAK!*"

CHAPTER TWENTY-SIX

I'm **dead,** the Toad thought.

But she didn't feel dead. She could still feel the floor beneath her and a cool, soft breeze that washed over her. Her eyes were closed and her brow furrowed. Slowly, warily, she winked open one eye, but only a little.

There was a brief moment of confusion as her waking mind shook off the lingering impressions of the dream.

"Father? Where am I?" She held up her small green hand and realized, *It was a dream, just a dream.*

"No," a voice said. "Not just a dream."

The Toad could see the floor. It was not that of the study. It looked as though it were made of some shimmering white, iridescent stone. It was cool and soothing. She turned slightly in the other direction and winked open her other eye...

and saw a slim, bare human foot that disappeared under the folds of a bone-colored gown with traces of golden patterns shifting in the dim light. The Toad quickly righted herself, realizing that she was no longer bound in spider silk.

"I am NoNe. I am the White Widow and Keeper of the Clock." She had a kind face, laced with deep wrinkles; her skin was paler than the bone gown she wore. Her long hair was platinum, fine as a spiderweb, and full and radiant with health. The strangest thing about her was her eyes. They looked like smooth, perfectly formed pearls.

"But...I thought I was going to die because I answered all the questions wrong and the Silver Widow bit me and—" She suddenly halted her rapid stream of words as her eyes came to rest on NoNe's face. "You're not a spider. You're...really, really"—she paused—"...old!"

"Yes," NoNe said, "I am. This is what happens when you live your life and successfully avoid getting killed." There was a note of amusement in her voice and she did not sound old at all.

NoNe lifted one outstretched hand to shoulder level and increased the brilliance of the room a hundredfold. The Toad gasped in awe. They were at the center of a vast crystalline web. It began in a radius not more than three hops away and stretched out into a blinding white forever in all directions. Small arcs of lightning raced along threads. Some threads were solid, others were clear. There were red threads, blue, yellow, green...every color that she could think of. Tiny glass spiders spun threads, but there were some being severed as well. When she saw those, she knew that someone, somewhere, had ended.

The Toad looked down at herself. "I'm not dead? I mean . . . of course I'm not dead . . . but the Silver Widow . . ."

"Silver's bite does not kill. It heals . . . among other things," NoNe said simply.

"You're not really human, are you?" the Toad said, looking up at her. "But you are speaking a human language."

NoNe merely looked at her with a slight smile.

"And I can understand you and talk to you," the Toad continued. "But it's different this time. I don't feel the magic. I don't feel like I'm translating. I feel like I'm . . ."

"Remembering," NoNe said.

"Remembering . . . yes . . ." the Toad repeated in a whisper, her eyes narrowing in thought. "And the dreams. Each time I was bit I dreamed of a girl but it didn't really feel like a dream. It also felt like I was . . ."

NoNe nodded at her, a half smile playing about her ancient face.

"Remembering," the Toad said. "And that means the girl in my dream is . . ."

"Many things, as are we all, but at this moment she is a toad."

"And if all that is true, that means"—the Toad paused, frowning—"my father is dead."

The White Widow regarded the Toad for a long moment. She seemed not only to be looking at the Toad, but looking

into her in much the same way Jack had done when they first met. And she felt just as vulnerable.

"It is time...Ask your question."

The Toad had a long list of questions and all of them seemed moderately important, at least to her. But now that her very own dreams had revealed her first question about her identity, there was really only one that stood above the rest and it sprang out of her almost immediately.

"I want to get out...How do I escape the Kitchen?"

NoNe shimmered for a moment and the Toad caught a fleeting, flickering glimpse of a huge arachnid, bearing a transparent carapace. Smoky shapes roiled within it. The shapes looked oddly familiar...almost like...faces.

And then NoNe was there again. Her hands stretched out in front of her, one palm up, the other palm down. She stood unmoving and unspeaking. Her face was an implacable void, as if she were no longer within herself.

Her voice seemed to come from everywhere at once:

"I don't know. Ask me something else."

CHAPTER TWENTY-SEVEN

hat?"

"I wouldn't be stuck in this clock if I knew how to escape the Kitchen, now would I?" NoNe said. "Do you think it's fun watching the threads of other people's lives day in and day out? Does that sound like a good job to you?" NoNe was shaking her head.

"But, but you're supposed to answer my question. I got bit! Three times!"

"I did answer your question...No one said that I was all-knowing, did they? I can't take the time to follow every single thread and find out what happens in every single life. Look at that web." NoNe pointed. "It would take forever. They all intertwine. They all twist around each other...it's impossible. It's hard enough to keep the threads intact for their allotted duration; they're extremely fragile."

"But Jack said you'd help."

The White Widow kneeled and said gently, "Haven't we? Each time you were bit, you received a memory. You know more now than when you came in, don't you?"

"Yes, but..."

NoNe held up her hand in a halting gesture. "Please understand if you delay, if you wait for answers to all your questions, you will wait forever. You will become the widow of your own web, an observer, rather than a participant in your own life.

"It's almost lunchtime," NoNe said. "Ask another question or be satisfied with what you have."

The Widows had given her some pieces of her memory and it was true, no one had said the White Widow would be able to answer any question.

"No, no more questions. I get it. I understand your lesson. I just wish it had involved less biting."

A loud chime sounded deep within the belly of the clock tower and suddenly the brilliance of the web flickered like a candle and went out. NoNe was gone and the Toad was once again in complete darkness.

"First question," a thick slurring voice issued from the darkness.

"But...wait..." The Toad had forgotten about the last part of her ordeal. "...Crud."

"Three questions up, one asked, now...three questions down.

"Ahem...Do you agree to release the Widows of the Clock from any acts of vengeance or vendetta as may be inspired by the knowledge gained within the clock, for all time, which is to say in perpetuity, not dependent upon a particular plane of existence or particular incarnation of said Widows?"

"Umm...Yes?" the Toad replied tentatively.

"Second question: Do you agree to never, under dire penalty, try to contact the Widows by any other means than the front access, meaning the brass plate, with the understanding that any form of nonphysical locomotion into or out of the clock may potentially tear space, thus causing the inevitable destruction of reality as it so stands?"

She didn't understand, but yes still seemed to be the right answer.

"Final question: Do you agree to refrain from discussing, whether in verbal, psychic, or magical discourse, the specifics of your admittance to, and subsequent trials in gaining the highest level of the clock?"

She looked toward the sound of the voice in the darkness and asked, "Does that mean I can't talk about what I've learned while here?"

"Nawww, just the part about the questions and gettin' bit an' all."

"Oh, then, yes."

"Handprint here, please," the voice commanded.

"I...I don't understand," she responded.

"Make your handprint here. Right here." The deep guttural voice was a bit impatient.

"I can't see anything. Where?" she said, confused.

"Oh...right...sorry." There was a small pop, a swooshing sound, and a spherical glass ball appeared above her head and began to emit a low steady glow.

A brown piece of parchment was thrust in her face as the light increased.

"Handprint here..." The big black spider tapped a blank line underneath the elegant script on the aged paper.

"I have no ink." The Toad was getting irritated.

"Come on, come on, ya got some blood in yer body, don't ya? Use that." He was losing patience as fast as the Toad was.

"I am not going to cut myself!" she said as she grabbed the parchment out of his hands.

She licked her right hand with her long, wet toad tongue, leaving a huge glob of saliva on her palm, and slapped it down on the old brown paper.

"There, that's what you get." And she handed the dripping manuscript back to the spider.

"I guess it'll have to do," the spider said in obvious distaste.

"I guess it will," she snapped back.

The spider rolled the parchment up and placed it into a leather bag and stepped back out of the low light, vanishing. The Toad stood there for a few moments, quite unsure of how to proceed. Thankfully the problem was solved when nearby, a familiar brass plate swung open.

Chuck ducked his head down into the entrance, looking at her. "You might want ta get out here," Chuck said. "Things is going on."

The Toad stepped out of the Widows' Clock, her night sight returning to her instantly. In the distance she saw Jack, Pug, and Sootfoot looking at something out of her sight on the ground and wearing expressions of repulsion and disdain. A contingent of sentry spiders surrounded them, looking at the same thing.

Jack waved her over. "You need to see this."

In the center of the circle was the crib that had been following her since the start of her journey in the Kitchen. It saw her and tried to click its beak, but it had been muzzled, with fairy braid no less. It was fitted like a leash. Horsefly stood holding the braid lightly, in one hand, not at all like someone who had hold of a dangerous creature.

"She won't let anyone near it. I assume she's waiting for you," Jack said.

The Toad hopped over.

The fairy jumped to her feet when she saw her, speaking quickly.

The Toad gasped. "It knows a way out!"

CHAPTER TWENTY-EIGHT

So...you're a human," Jack said. "And a shape changer."

"Yes. It looks that way," the Toad said. "I don't have all my memories and what I do have, it's like they happened to someone else."

"Well, that explains a few things, don't it?" said Pug.

"It does," Jack nodded.

"It's no wonder you don't eat meat," Sootfoot said.

"That's right," Jack said. "Shape changers that haven't imprinted their First Form can't be near living animals, and nor can they consume them." He paused. "Your father. Mirabella did a real wicked job on you and yours, didn't she?"

"An' this thing..." Pug hooked a thumb at the small skeletal bird. "It really has a way out?"

"That's what Horsefly says," the Toad said. "And I believe her. I think this crib has been following me. I believe this is the pet falcon that I was made to let go of in my fourth year, Bibbett. But there's only one way to know..."

She walked over to the crib and loosened the makeshift muzzle. She squatted in front of the little bone bird and began to sing a song, one from her early childhood.

An interesting thing happened to the Toad at that moment. She began to see the crib differently. She could see a form over the skeleton, flesh and feather. The Toad was seeing the bird as it had been when it was alive, its silver-and-grey-tipped feathers resting transparently over bone. So, too, did its rapid clicks become chirps and warbles. It was singing back to her. The crib cocked its skull sideways and leaned against her, rubbing its bony brow against her shoulder as a dog might do.

She realized that she was beginning to understand the chirps and that it must have been trying to speak to her for quite some time, perhaps from the very beginning. Once she realized this, it only took a few moments for her to translate its meaning.

The chirps and warbles were very much like the sounds that the trolls had made—emotional rather than literal. She could not say it out loud, it was too sad: *When will I fly again?* Bibbett asked.

The fairy began to speak and the Toad translated. "I knew of the cribis from the Leaper's tale of escaping the

Witch's cauldron. When I saw it at StillBright Hollow I knew it to be odd for a cribis, but in a different way than the blackened birds, the altered crines. It was not attached to the Sisters as the others are. After the battle at Still-Bright Hollow, I decided to examine its magic. I followed it for a time and it led me to a spiker, a pinfetcher nest. It dove in. After a time the spiker came to roost. I waited. The spiker left the nest and I looked in, and it began to swirl like water, inside at its base. After a moment the cribis emerged. I roped it. Though truly, it did not fight as its brethren would have done. I found your path, what remained of it, from StillBright...you are not a stealthy lot."

"How did she know that the portal led outside the Kitchen?" Sootfoot asked.

The Toad related the question to Horsefly, who merely reached under her sword strap and produced a leaf of brilliant green.

"Wha's that? Never seen it before," Pug said.

"It's a greenfen leaf," Jack said, eyebrow raising. "That's good proof. Greenfen doesn't grow in shadow."

The fairy handed the leaf to Jack and spoke again.

She said, "It smells like outside...does it not?"

Jack doubted the fairy had ever been "outside" the Kitchen but he placed the leaf to his nose and inhaled, then nodded his head in agreement.

The fairy turned to address the Toad directly. "You are a human, yes? You have told me this?"

"Um...yes," the Toad said, caught off guard by Horsefly's direct question.

"You will not leave until you have returned my sword."

The Toad couldn't tell if this was a question or a statement but, she thought, perhaps it was both. She replied, "I will not leave until you have yours."

It's time at least to try, the Toad thought and sat down on the ground. *This is as good a place as I'm likely to get.*

Horsefly's blade. I can't leave until I retrieve it. I hadn't yet been taught the discipline of Calling when Mirabella caught me. Summoning a lost possession is supposed to be extremely difficult, but I did send it away easy enough.

She thought about the second sword, remembering the fight with the water wrath and how the fairy had danced her way around the creature. She had been so whole and complete in her spinning and whirling. The Toad wanted more than anything to return that feeling to the fairy. It was horrible when you were missing a part of yourself. Now that she had recovered some of her own missing parts, her memories and Bibbett, she understood that even more.

She looked at Jack, who was sitting quietly and examining a large stone, half-embedded in the floor. "Are you gonna sculpt something outta that?" she asked.

His eye had the look of someone who had just surfaced from some deep thought. "Maybe, it depends." He placed his iron palm on the stone.

"Is it like you're seeing what could be made out of the material?" she asked.

"Yeah, kinda," Jack answered, "what could be...and what should be."

The Toad contemplated Horsefly. "Fight," she said.

The fairy cocked her head and gave her a quizzical look.

"Pretend to fight...as if you had both your blades."

"Ahhh," Horsefly said, "I am to practice the sword dance."

"Yes, exactly."

Horsefly began to move in half circles, slowly at first. She held her one blade in her right hand and moved her left as if the second blade were present. It was difficult but soon she had adjusted her balance to account for the imaginary sword and she began making graceful spinning arcs.

The Toad watched and as she did she imagined that she too could feel the swords in Horsefly's hands—both of them. She allowed herself to become enthralled in the hypnotic movements of the dance. Horsefly continued and soon Jack, Pug, and Sootfoot were watching as well.

"What's this?" Sootfoot asked.

"SSSHHHH!" Pug said a bit more insistently than he meant to.

Jack was simply smiling and nodding.

The Toad watched the dance, and her eyes were sharp and focused. In her mind she allowed herself to see what could have been there in Horsefly's empty hand, or, as Jack had said, what should have been there.

It happened so suddenly and so naturally that it took

Horsefly a moment to realize that her blade had returned. She spun three times before she slowed and stopped the dance, staring at the blade that had quietly materialized into existence in her left hand.

Horsefly stared at the twin swords for but a heartbeat and then began to secure them on her back straps. She did not shed a single tear, but she did smile...a little.

"Now," she said to the Toad, "you may leave."

≋

"Sorry as hell we can't go with ya, mate," Chuck said to Jack as he and his two silent spider friends escorted the small troop of strange companions to the edge of the clearing.

They all paused at the edge of the grass. One more step and they would be back on the stone floor of the Kitchen. The Kitchen that had actively tried to kill them just a few hours ago.

"Is it safe again?" she asked. "I mean...like it was before it tried to flatten us."

"Can't say," Jack answered. "Looks okay. The path has parted again." But no one made a move. Horsefly turned and looked at them with a raised eyebrow. She shook her head, shrugged slightly, and stepped onto the cold stone floor. She paced back and forth for a moment...nothing happened. She looked at the small band of travelers and said, *"Meneri seraferish eh..."*

The Toad chuckled. "Let's go. Horsefly says it's safe enough."

"Safe enough for what?" Soot asked.

"Safe enough for meekmice."

"That's as good as it's gonna get," Jack said.

And with that, they all joined Horsefly.

The fairy pointed at the crib but the Toad had already let out some lead on its leash. Bibbett clicked at her once and began to move forward.

It was really an unusual sight, even for a place as wondrous and chaotic as the Kitchen: a crib, on a leash held by a Toad, followed closely by a fairy and an imp, and two Wickerfolk bringing up the rear. They continued for perhaps a dozen or so stone and when the tension did not diminish, the Toad was the first to speak.

"Jack?" she started. "I don't want to sound like a scared rabbit, but something feels wrong."

"What's wrong?" Pug said from behind. "D'ya see sumthin' up there?"

"It's not what she's seeing," Jack said. "It's what she's not hearing."

The Kitchen was silent. Not just silent but dead still. The Toad stopped moving and listened more closely. There were no sounds. No sounds of shuffling, scurrying, or anything else for that matter.

"Jack..." she said. "The Kitchen isn't moving...at all."

CHAPTER TWENTY-NINE

**had always labored** under the assumption that the Kitchen was random in its movements," Sootfoot said from the back of the party. "But recent events have forced me to conclude otherwise."

"The Sisters made this place. Caused it to be," Jack said. "But they've never shown this kind of control over it."

"Could Grisswell do it? Could it be another trap?" the Toad asked.

"Maybe. His power is...terrible. But this isn't his style. He's not subtle," Jack answered. "Whatever's going on, we should keep moving. How far is the pinfetcher nest anyway?"

"Horsefly says it's less than one hundred and thirty stone if her direction holds true. And this little guy will take us right to it." She reached over and ruffled feathers that no one else could see.

Bibbett made a hop, straining at his leash and pulling her with him.

"Jack," the Toad began, "I wonder how Bibbett's essence survived its transformation into a crib."

"Yeah, I've been thinking about that and I have a theory," he said. "Sometimes those with shape-changing abilities can magically imprint animals if they're not careful. Something passed between you and Bibbett."

"Oh, yeah ... I see. We shared a spark and you think it somehow bound us together all this time?" the Toad said.

"It would explain why the Witches had a hard time controlling him. He already had a master. One that he was not only bound to magically, but also loved."

The Toad nodded her agreement and gave Bibbett a long, gentle stroke on the side of his head.

The silence was nerve-racking after the Toad had become so used to the constant, low shuffling of the items in the Kitchen. The furnishings weren't the only things not moving. There hadn't been a glimpse of another living creature, outside of their own party, since they set foot on the floor.

As they made their way, the Toad looked up at Jack. "Will you tell me about Grisswell now?"

"I guess ..." he said, but it was obvious that he didn't want to.

"What is this Vow that he wants you to take? What does it mean?" she asked.

"It's called the Vow of Excision. All demons eventually have to take it," Jack replied flatly.

"What do you mean 'all demons'?" she asked, her brow knitted in confusion.

"Imps are immature demons," Sootfoot said from behind. He said it as if it were a simple fact, common knowledge.

"It's true," Jack said. "All imps are immature demons."

"What? But my aunt told me about imps and she never said anything about..." But Jack interrupted her.

"Humans barely know that we exist at all. How could any of them know that imps don't stay imps forever? Those that have had the odd exchange with an imp would never have cause to suspect that we are anything more than what we appear to be. Beings of low and middle magic, for the most part, are harmless," Jack continued. "My father is a full demon; so is my mother. They have been for ten thousand years. My father's the reason the Witches were able to capture me and try to steal my talents." After a long pause, Jack, while looking out into the dark, said, "He gave me to them because he despised my artistic inclinations."

"Your... your father gave you to them?"

"He's furious that I'm not a full demon yet. He decided that if the Witches stole my gifts, then I would have nothing keeping me from becoming a full demon. When an imp reaches the age of inclusion, usually around three hundred years old, they are marked and made to recite the Vow of Excision. The Vow gives the imp enormous power and magical ability, but the cost is separation from any feelings of belonging, compassion, or love. Anything decent within the imp is burned out and charred, left with nothing but anger and rage."

"Why would anyone do that?" she asked.

"Power."

"Ughh!!" she said, her eyes wide with revulsion. "That's just insane. What good is power if all you can do is destroy? I mean, what's the point?"

Jack thought for a second and said, "I agree with you, but there are those that think power gives them control. Most imps aren't like me; they spend their entire childhood waiting for the time until they can take the Vow. Some aspire to take over the human realm and the more power they gather the better chance they have. But what would you do with it? Would you have everyone bow to you, bring you offerings? Boring. Really, being malicious and constantly evil would be tedious, not to mention lonely. Everyone would always be out to knock you off your throne and steal your stuff. Plus, if I became a demon I would be at the bottom of the hierarchy and be forced to serve. My demonic powers would add to my mother's and father's might and I would be their slave... until I either slew them or betrayed them to another Kethish lord."

"Wait, so where's your mother?"

"She outranks my father in the demonic hierarchy so I'm his responsibility. It's another reason why he wants to turn me. If he does he could equal her in standing."

"It doesn't make any sense to me." The Toad shook her head in disgust.

"I'm not sure that it actually makes sense to anyone but demons, but that's how it's always been." Jack looked very solemn.

"So all imps become demons, always?"

"Well, there have been others, to be sure, that have gone against the grain and never taken the Vows but there haven't been many. In my lifetime I have known only one other."

"And?" she asked.

"And what?"

"And what happened to him, the other one that stayed an imp?" she asked.

"Oh...he's dead."

"They killed him!?" Her eyes were wide with shock.

"No, no, no." He held up his hand and made the "keep your voice down" gesture, though it was more out of habit. There wasn't anything around to notice whether they made noise or not.

"He was accidentally eaten by a forest wyvern that mistook him for a hairless gopher."

"Oh...oh..." She hadn't realized that she had stopped walking until Bibbett tugged against the leash. "Well, that's horrible, too."

Sootfoot, who had been listening intently, spoke up. "And is that why you stay in the Kitchen?"

"Who, me? Nooo, I know how to handle a wyvern," he said, smiling.

Sootfoot did not return the smile and merely stared at him blankly.

"You can leave!?" She stopped walking again.

Jack sighed and then nodded. "It's true. I can leave. Whenever I want. All I have to do is cut out my heart by taking the oath."

The Toad looked at him with a confused expression. "But I thought you were trying to escape like me... with me."

Jack looked at her earnestly. "I will do everything I can to help you get outta here, and if I can throw a big snag in whatever misbegotten plans those two Witches have cooked up, then all the better, but I can't leave with you. The magic of the Kitchen keeps me hidden. No one can find me in here. Sure, if I wanted to leave I could walk out the front door, but it wouldn't be me who came through on the other side. The 'me' that walked through those doors is no one that you would ever want to hang out with."

Jack reached up and took off his cap. The two hidden eyes blinked open. "The middle eye sees the pain that people cause each other," he said. "The top eye"—he paused—"sees the wretchedness within. If I were to become a true demon these eyes would never be shut again."

The Toad looked down; she hadn't wanted to let him see how upset she was.

"I didn't know any of this. I just thought..." She paused and looked up at him. "But Jack, Grisswell did find you...back at the pass."

"I know. I haven't figured that one out yet," he said, pulling his cap down over his closing eyes.

CHAPTER THIRTY

The crib led the Toad, who like-wise led the rest. Horsefly and Jack assumed their usual roles as lookout and bodyguard, though it was hard to tell which was which. Pug started humming the melodies of some off-color drinking songs and Sootfoot was determined to continue his attempts to master the flute. He silently practiced his finger placement and put the flute to his lips occasionally, but Jack still constantly cautioned him against trying to sound it.

They came to the pinfetcher nest without event, which was a quite unusual feat in itself. Nothing tried to eat, kill, detain, restrain, or otherwise maim any of them.

The nest was only a little taller than the one the Toad had fallen into, which was about chest-high to Jack. Horsefly walked up the tangle of thorns, pieces of glass, and pins as

if she were climbing a tree. She stood at the top of the nest looking in. The pinfetcher was absent. Most likely off on some "pointed" mission of its own.

"Well, here we are," Jack said.

"Great. Now what? I can't just dive through with Bibbett," the Toad said.

"Most likely, that's exactly what you have to do," Jack replied.

After a long pause the Toad looked up at Horsefly. "I guess this would be the right time to ask: Who's going to go?" she said.

Sootfoot was the first to answer. "I will go with you, if you'll allow me. I wasn't born in the Kitchen as my friend Pug here. I'd really prefer to see daylight again."

"I been in the Kitchen for as long as I can remember. If there's an outside where everything don't always try ta eat ya, I'm fer it," Pug said. "I may not be much help, but I can cook. Even if it's just veggies and greens."

The Toad looked up at Horsefly and the fairy spoke quickly. "We are orphans. And sisters. Better than the Witches." She paused, shaking her head. "And you are still wild with magic. You have found your memories but you have not yet found yourself. I will go."

Though she dreaded to look into his face because she knew what his answer would be, she turned to Jack.

He was looking away. His entire posture was slouched and sorrowful and his hands were thrust into his pockets.

"Jack..." she started.

"I can't," he said quietly. "I want to...but I just can't."

"What if we fought..."

"Grisswell? Not possible." He shook his head. "Full demons are...they're just too strong. You saw what happened when you blasted him with your magic—Ancient magic. He barely noticed. The only reason the Witches can command him is because they did him a favor in capturing me. He works for them until I make the Vow."

Jack turned to look at her. His eye was sparkling but not with magic or mirth. It glistened with a tear.

She had been through a great deal on this journey, but this was the hardest thing by far. It's one thing to risk your life but it's another to watch someone risk theirs for you and then to walk away from them, probably forever.

Letting go of Bibbett's braided leash, she threw her small arms around Jack's leg and squeezed him with all her might.

Jack wiped his eye and smiled. He reached into his pocket and pulled out the stone carving he'd worked on while she was in the clock. He had fashioned a neck strap from a piece of Horsefly's fairy braid.

"This is for you," he said and placed it around her stubby green neck. "I made it when you were in the clock. It's not magic or anything, except for the braid. It'll stay on you even if things get rough through the portal."

"Oh, Jack. The carving, it's incredible. It's..." And as she studied the form that Jack's talent had wrought from the piece of common stone her eyes widened in amazement. "Beautiful!"

It was the face of a girl. Though the carving was rough, she displayed strong smooth features and a slender upturned nose. The shape of her hair fell, full and rolling, around her face.

"I couldn't get the detail any finer than that. Not with these things"—he wiggled his iron fingers at her—"but I thought you would like it."

"It looks so, so familiar!" she said as she turned it slowly in her hands.

Jack looked back and forth from her to the carving. "You know, I thought the same thing."

"I'll keep it forever. I swear it." She held it in her hand, studying it. She thought it grew warm under her touch.

"Leave now?" Horsefly called from the top of the pinfetcher nest.

"I guess it's that time," the Toad said.

She turned to Bibbett and pointed to the nest. It clicked at her once and, having no flesh or feathers to snag on the jagged edges, it raced up the side of the structure in leaps and bounds. The skeletal bird paused at the top of the nest and looked back, waiting for her.

"Have Pug hold the leash as the crib leaps through. Fairy braid is shallow magic but it should keep the portal from closing long enough for the rest of you to get through," Jack said.

Pug carefully made his way up the side of the nest. After a few mishaps and swearwords he was standing next to Horsefly.

"It's working!" Pug said as he looked down into the center of the pinfetcher's construction.

The bottom of the nest had started to waver not unlike the fairy fire, producing no heat. By the time the Toad had made her way up the side, yelping every time her tender white belly hit a needle, the interior of the nest was moving in a slow spiral. Bibbett stood at the edge of the movement. The little bird creature looked up at the Toad and then dove into the center of the motion, instantly disappearing. The fairy braid drew taut, as if something was dangling on the other side like a fish on a line.

The Toad stood on the edge and waited for Sootfoot, who was having a greater degree of difficulty, mainly because his jack legs were not built for climbing, and he insisted on keeping his flute in one hand at all times.

Twice he almost fell and twice Jack reached out and gave him a boost. "Thank you, Jack," Sootfoot said as he finally reached the top. "After you two. I insist."

The fairy, not one to err on the side of caution, did a near-perfect swan dive and disappeared as well.

Not wasting any time, the Toad turned and gave a parting smile at Jack and then stepped into the portal.

A cold, solid blackness and weightlessness met her inside. There was a brief feeling of horrifyingly fast acceleration that ended with a sound like a bursting wineskin.

She was propelled out of the portal and landed on the stone floor in a tumble. The Toad scrambled to her feet and found that she was standing very close to a regular bird's nest. Horsefly reached over and slid the fairy braid off the bird's neck and tied it to a twig protruding from the edge of the nest. Then she and the Toad took a deep breath and looked around.

As Sootfoot hurtled through and landed with a thud next to her, she knew ... knew beyond a shadow of a doubt.

This was definitely not "outside."

hey had emerged from the portal and landed in what appeared to be a small ramshackle room. And they weren't alone. Standing all around were figures, unmoving and hard to make out in the darkness, even with her night sight. She could see them, but they just didn't seem...right.

The fairy drew one of her swords and touched the tip of the blade, making a spark of light that burned dim but constant.

"*Emanari nosisari,*" she said. "Not living."

"Are those what I think they are?" the Toad said as her eyes adjusted to the dim luminescence. "Yes," she answered her own question, "they're dolls." And looking around she added, "We're in a dollhouse. A weird doll-house, but that's what it is. Look, there's a little table and a broken cup."

"It still smells, still feels like we're in the Kitchen," Sootfoot said as he clutched his flute tightly.

"We are," she replied. "What happened? What went wrong?" the Toad asked as she paced a circle around the nest.

Horsefly shook her head in consternation.

Bibbett huddled down next to the nest and was still, which did not fill the Toad with good feelings. Rather, it unnerved her. Since meeting the little crib, it had not been silent or still. Till now.

As Sootfoot righted himself and got to his feet, she asked, "Where's Pug?"

"Jack said he should pause for a moment to make sure that nothing was amiss, before following," Sootfoot said. "I see that it was good advice. Where are we, exactly?"

The Toad looked around, squinting her eyes and trying to extract details in the darkness. She made a small hop forward and looked between the mismatched boards of the walls of the dollhouse. Her eyes suddenly widened and she tumbled backward: "Quick, get back! *Go back into the portal!*"

"Why, what in the world is wrong?" Sootfoot asked, alarmed and moving back toward the nest.

"That's the door! The front door! This thing is just sitting right in front of the front door! It's a trap!!!"

A familiar voice seeped from the darkness. "It was a trap. Now it's sprung. You didn't think that I would not know the comings and goings of my own Kitchen? You really are a stupid child," Emilina said evenly. "Here we are, all of us, and just in time."

The Toad looked up, eyes wide in horror as the flat roof of the patchwork dollhouse was lifted and taken away. The tall, reed-thin woman appeared above them and stared down at her. Though her voice had been relatively expressionless, she wore a glaring, hateful sneer on her face. In her left hand she held a familiar black book.

"And you've brought friends to our tea party, how nice," she continued. "You do like tea, don't you, dear?" She held her right hand palm up and made a small waving gesture that caused the structure to rise up off the floor and float close to her face. "And I see the wretched crib took the greenfen leaves from the front gate, that I placed in the dollhouse as bait. How marvelous."

Before any of them could recover from their shock enough to make it through the nest, Emilina closed her hand into a fist and smashed it down upon the dollhouse. The whole thing crashed to the floor and broke apart. The nest rolled on its side a short distance away; doll parts flew everywhere, not to mention the Toad and Sootfoot. The only one who landed on her feet was the fairy.

A strange sputtering sound filled the air and even Emilina paused.

Rolling over onto her feet, the Toad looked up to see Sarafina standing not a stone's throw away, shaking, trembling with either rage or sorrow. Most likely both, but to be quite honest, with her face it was very difficult to tell.

Nearby Horsefly was standing with one sword held at a diagonal across the front of her slender body, the other blade still strapped to her back. With her free hand she was beginning a gesture of magic. She threw it at Emilina, who was distracted, pointedly ignoring Sarafina.

A small ball of fairy fire erupted inside Emilina's left eye. The eye smoldered for a brief second then exploded outward in a shower of ooze, which pattered on the floor like rain.

The Witch did not seem to feel it at all. She merely raised her hand and wiped the viscous fluid from her cheek. When she removed her hand the eye had returned as if it had never been gone. Only now the iris was a putrid yellowish color, a creepy mismatch to her darker right eye.

"What a charming little spell. I shall have to make note of it. I may need to inconvenience someone with it one day."

Horsefly drew her second blade, but before she could take so much as a single step a sound sprang up and filled the air. Sootfoot's flute. But instead of the inconsistent screeching sound he had produced in the past, a long pure note rang out. It was beautiful and perfect and it worked perfectly. The Toad and Horsefly stood frozen like two odd little figurines in a strange dance.

"Soot, my pet. Well done, well done. I was beginning to have my doubts about you. 'Virtuoso' was the word you used to describe yourself, was it not? Perhaps that was a bit...generous, but at least the flute works as it was intended. It did give you some control over the Kitchen, did it not?"

Sootfoot made an attempt at a flourished bow. His movements were awkward and jerky, not at all like his normal self.

"Yes, Mistress Emilina. I pretended to practice, but unknown to the others, I played the silent notes that kept the path under control." Sootfoot spoke without emotion or expression. All of his bright intellectual bearing and conviviality had vanished. This dullish creature was not at all the character that the Toad had grown fond of along the path.

"And they kept us posted as to your location as well. Sarafina made significant improvements to the flute and hid them well."

"Yes, miss, everyone who cared to look saw only a spiralsong. They had no idea that it was anything more."

"Her magic is competent at times," Emilina said.

There was a derisive snort from somewhere behind the Toad, a deep, gurgling sound that came from a deep, gurgling throat. "You're too kind to me, Sister," Sarafina chuffed. "I am most embarrassed by the praise." Her voice was still hard from the destruction of her dollhouse.

"Not to worry, Sister," Emilina chided. "It isn't likely to happen soon again."

Another snort from Sarafina.

"But we do have what we need now and that is indeed thrilling, isn't it?" Emilina continued. "The cauldron has begun to stir. The time is very close."

226

Something was very close. And even though she couldn't move, the Toad could sense a force, like a gathering storm, beginning to collect all around them. It made her skin crawl with panic, compounding the claustrophobia of paralysis. Her colors were beginning to shift. And it wasn't going unnoticed.

"Oh, look," Emilina said in a rather bored fashion. "The little Toad is trying to use magic. Sister, will you please?"

She heard the movement behind her, but there was nothing she could do as the red velvet sack was pulled over her head and jostled her body as it crept under her feet.

The sack was powerful. It positively thrummed with magic.

I can move again, she realized. The bag was meant to contain her power but it also nullified the effects of Sootfoot's flute. She could feel the magic but she couldn't send it through the thin walls of the sack. *Can I do anything?* Her mind raced.

"The girl has grown in power in her short time here," Sarafina said.

"The poison had a great deal to do with that, Sister," Emilina spat the words, growing instantly irritated. "It was made improperly."

"It bloody well wasn't!" Sarafina bit back. "How was I to know that she had channels to the Deep River in her bloodline? It was only meant to speed her to First Form. You never told me that she was the first girl in her lineage in ten generations. If I had known the last female born had been gifted with Second Form attributes, then the elixir would have been remixed to account for the possibility."

"So you say." Emilina grew cool once again. "At least the containment spell invested in the bag still seems to work."

"Seems to work? Of course it works. It took three years to make and nearly turned out to be the death of me. 'Seems to work,' FAH!" Sarafina said. "It's no easy task to trap magic in a sack! The magic within, stays within. The magic without, stays without."

"But it would have been more useful if we could cast into the bag from this side. It blocks our power as well," Emilina said. "Perhaps next time we shall try to think ahead, yes?"

Sarafina huffed in response.

"Cauldron. Place yourself here," Emilina pointed to a large clear spot on the floor.

The cauldron was perhaps the only item that the Sisters had possessed longer than the Book. When Sarafina had acquired the thing, it was already ancient and encrusted with centuries of use. It had grown in power as a magical vessel over the years and had developed a limited intelligence of its own. It had also, like many of their servants, developed a great fear of the Sisters.

The large four-legged pot trotted over and sank to the floor, shaking on its haunches. Its contents swirled of their own accord. A putrid green glow was beginning to seep out.

"What are we going to do with this...pest?" Sarafina asked, nodding toward the fairy.

"She'll go in the cauldron after the Toad. The pot will channel her magic as well. It won't last long in us, but we'll take it and use it, for what it's worth," Emilina said.

Inside the bag she couldn't see anything, but the Toad was listening. *Did she say that someone in my family was Second Form? That can't be,* she thought. *Father mentioned Second Form only once...*

"It's not something to concern yourself with, dear," she remembered him saying to her. *"There hasn't been Second Form in...oh, I'd say three hundred years. But as legends go, Second Forms are truly inspiring. They were throwbacks to the Ancient Deep River, the most powerful magic that had existed on the mortal plane. Shape changers in the broadest sense. One of our ancestors, the sorceress Illucidale, was such a one. She could not only assume the First Form of her totem animal but any form that she had cause to study. And her shape-changing prowess was not limited to herself, as we are today, but she could change others, as well as nonliving things. Why, there is even one tale, as preposterous as it may seem, wherein she was reputed to have changed the shape of time itself...and her with no formal disciplines. She was all self-taught."*

"It's almost time to send for Grisswell," Emilina said. "Sarafina, make yourself useful. Destroy that nest before that insufferable crib escapes you again."

Sarafina walked over to the nest. The crib lay huddled

on the floor beside it. She gently picked up the small skeletal bird, smiling at it thinly as it lifted its head and clicked
at her. "You naughty, naughty little...Aaaaiiieee!" she
squealed as Bibbett's needle-sharp beak pierced the meaty
flesh between her thumb and forefinger.

She dropped the crib to the floor, raised her foot, and
stomped it into a pile of dust. The black marble shot out
from the force of the blow. It made a *tink, tink, tink* sound
as it bounced off into the darkness.

Emilina rolled her eyes at her sister. "Can you manage
the nest, or might that attack you as well?"

The bullish woman growled and grumbled as she hefted
herself to a crouch to pick up the nest, huffing all the way.
She prepared to destroy her most prized possession, but she
couldn't stop herself from looking into the bowl of its knitted, interlacing twigs and small branches one last time.

"But it's so beaut..." Sarafina froze in mid-sentence. A
large green eye was staring out of the center of the nest. It
blinked at her and, perhaps for the first time in her adult
life, she squealed in fear.

"EEEEEEEEPPPPPPPP!!!!"

Her squeal turned into a true scream as Natterjack's
head launched out of the nest and bit her hard on the hand.
Sarafina stumbled, tried to jerk away from his battening
teeth, but all she succeeded in doing was extracting the
rest of the imp from the nest. Neck, shoulders, arms, torso,
hips, legs, and feet in one great pull.

For a brief moment Jack was dangling, held fast by his

teeth, from the meaty flesh of Sarafina's right hand. She dropped the nest and batted at him with her left. Her first attempt missed him entirely but she balled her hand into a fist and caught him solid with her second. Jack went flying through the air...and not in a graceful acrobatic way. More like an imp who's just taken a good shot to the breadbasket.

The nest rolled for a moment and came to rest upside down. Which, as it turned out, was a bit of luck. Pug was the last to come through the portal and the only one to make it through unseen. He hid under the delicate lattice of twigs, determined that this was not his sort of fight, not in the least. He probably would have stayed there, but something caught his eye. His friend Sootfoot was hiding, too, under a sideboard barely a stone's distance away. He saw what his furry friend was up to and he smiled.

Jack wasn't out for the nod. He didn't lose consciousness but he wasn't feeling too well at the moment either. He staggered up onto all fours, trying not to retch.

"Sootfoot, play Natterjack a tune, if you don't mind?" And even though Emilina's words were friendly, her tone was definitely not.

Sootfoot began to raise the flute to his lips and the smile melted from Pug's face. "So it's like that, is it?" he said to himself.

Just as the flute began to sound, Pug launched himself into his jack-legged friend and knocked the flute from his hand.

Sootfoot reeled from the impact and landed on his back. "What's wrong with you, Pug? Why did you hit me?" he asked. He reached for his flute, which had begun crawling back to him like an undulating worm.

Jack had barely made it to his feet when Emilina apparently grew tired of waiting for Sootfoot to respond. She threw a spell, which struck his body, full and direct.

Imps are particularly resistant to magic. This particular imp was exceptionally resistant to magic, mostly because of the massive amount of iron that he carried with him at all times. Iron, as a matter of magical fact, had a tendency to disrupt spells cast upon it, while at the same time augmenting spells cast with it. It was ironic that the nature of Emilina's curse was the one thing that diminished her ability to do damage to him and maximized his ability to do damage to her. It was a rare case of lack of foresight for her. That being said, Emilina's spell caused Jack's skin to prickle and spike with jabs of fiery pain. If his iron hands had not disrupted a portion of her spell it might very well have ended him then and there.

But he turned quickly and retaliated. Gouts of emerald-green impish flame erupted from Jack and totally enveloped Emilina, catching her completely off guard. But she had defenses of her own that more than equaled Jack's iron hands. She had the Book. And it had her.

The flame sizzled and popped. The surrounding tables and miscellaneous furnishings burned and charred, but Emilina did not. It was as if the Book inhaled the flame as it touched her. Not so much as a single hair on her head was singed, and Emilina smiled.

A voice from the deepest shadow echoed around them...

"Jackal...it iss time to come home."

Emilina looked up into the darkness that had begun swirling above their heads. "Grisswell, come and deal with your child," she said. "He's misbehaving."

CHAPTER THIRTY-TWO

"Like HELL!" Jack said.

He made a heroic effort to appear unaffected by Grisswell's approach, but he still dropped into a defensive crouch and made his huge hands into fists.

Jack lunged to one side of the cauldron and in anger he picked up a chair, hurling it at Emilina's head.

She was not a particularly agile woman, nor was she particularly amused as the leg of the chair caught her on the cheek, sending her reeling backward against a cabinet.

Jack had found her weakness. The Book couldn't protect her from physical attacks. He wasn't finished with her yet. Before she had the time to do more than blink, he loosed a small, iron-banded keg at her.

The keg was made of heavy wood and caught her

solidly in the midsection. Emilina made a coughing "WHOOOFFFF!!" sound as she doubled over.

Jack was reaching for another chair when two ham-size hands lifted him by the shoulders and flung him through the air. As he sailed, he caught the glimpse of the column of darkness beginning to form.

Grisswell was almost here.

Sarafina had thrown him high and hard, but Jack was as agile as Emilina was not. He turned in the air like a cat and landed, skidding on his hands and feet.

Sarafina was upon him, instantly grabbing him by the torso and lifting him into the air again, but this time he was facing her. Jack began to make a gesture of magic and at the last second...he punched Sarafina hard in the face.

The woman's head rocked back on her neck and two bloody teeth flew out of her mouth. She lowered her head and looked Jack in the eye. She was smiling a bloody smile.

"As's a good punch," she said, lisping through the holes of the missing teeth. She lifted him higher, and suddenly slammed him straight down onto the floor.

Jack couldn't move, or breathe. All he could do at that moment was lay there and try not to pass out. Luckily he hadn't hit headfirst or he would probably be considerably shorter than he already was—or dead.

As the darkness began to thicken, as the black portal began to coalesce, Emilina straightened herself and began a very intricate spell. She was not about to let Jack get away without a parting shot.

Jack was struggling to his feet as she finished and let it fly. Emilina spoke as the spell sped at Jack. Within the red velvet bag, the Toad heard the magical language and understood its meaning at once. Only three words, but carrying ancient power. Only three...

"You...are...undone!"

Jack's metal hands and forearms exploded and fell into pieces on the floor. He stood looking down at the shards of iron, his face a mingled expression of horror and disbelief.

"It will be quite hard to fight or sculpt without arms, won't it, Jackal? But really, in a few moments that won't matter anymore, will it?" Emilina said.

Grisswell stepped into the Kitchen accompanied by the sound of dark lightning and the howling of frigid winds. When he saw Jack standing wide-eyed with shock and confusion, the stumps of his arms waving in the air, the demon began to laugh.

"The Sisters play a very rough match with thee, child. And I see they have contained the Toad." His clawed hand gestured at the bag lying on the floor.

Jack looked at the small red bundle and his face wilted. It was a look of utter defeat, out of place on Nathaniel Jackard Heartswallow.

"Heart Render...Jackal...my child...come and be what you are meant to be. Leave this place and this pain." Grisswell opened his arms in a welcoming gesture that on anyone else might have seemed warm and inviting, but on him...well, the shiny black claws made it less accommodating.

Jack stood where he was, but the demon, as demons will, came to him. Grisswell crouched and hooked an enormous fingertip under Jack's chin. He slowly turned the imp around so that they were both facing the same direction. Grisswell bowed his head and began a deep, bonechilling chant.

Jack changed. The moment that Grisswell began to speak, the emerald color had leaked from Jack's large eye, turning a yellow, glowing amber. His skin became mottled, black and grey. Horned barbs and spikes tore out of him at his joints and along his back, down the ridge of his spine. His cap exploded into ash as bloodred horns grew like ivy, spiraling out of his skull. His hidden eyes opened wide and became as black as coal. His face narrowed and became a cruel snarl as his forearms began to regenerate, not of iron this time, but a deep red scaled skin that ended in black-tipped, hooked claws...not suitable for painting... or sculpting...or anything but tearing.

As the demon finished chanting he paused for a moment to survey his handiwork.

Jack let loose a soul-ripping, howling roar. Everyone who could manage it, even Grisswell himself, covered their ears. It seemed to wind out forever and finally when he exhausted his breath, the young demon stood, baring new fangs and panting like his namesake. He was Jackal, in form if not in spirit.

"I won't do it," Jack said. His voice was guttural, but still recognizable.

"Idiot child. I have given thee the demons' form and power. It will fester in you like an infection, waiting. How long before your mind is consumed by the fires of rage or corrupted by the desire to use your new abilities? Then, you will take the Vow." Grisswell laughed. "The longer thou resist, the more complete my victory. You will live in tortured agony, unable to seek the solace of death, for thou art Kethish now, at least in body, and the Keth kill, but do not die."

"I didn't recite the Vows. I am not Kethish. This is not binding," Jack growled.

"It is binding enough. Without the Vow, you may not have full demonic powers, but you have the form now, a form that calls to you. How unfair for thee this is." Grisswell chuckled. "Tradition asks that you recite the Vow upon your own volition, and I would have waited an age for you to do so, but"—Grisswell turned toward the Witches—"the Sisters would have slain thee if I had not come hence, for you were impish and still vulnerable. I could not permit the loss of such a servant as thee. Were they not protected"—he glanced at Emilina's Book—"I would consume them."

Emilina merely raised an eyebrow but did not speak.

"Our covenant is broken." With that Grisswell spun blindingly fast and grabbed Jack by the throat, his serrated claws digging into the scaled flesh. The father said to the son, "Your power will increase my power. Your rage will serve my rage."

He began walking toward the black portal.

Jack struggled against him, his own claws ripping and tearing at Grisswell, but to no avail. Grisswell was too powerful.

Just as they reached the edge of the portal, Jack stopped fighting and went limp.

"There, there, child. Let me comfort thee." Grisswell's mouth widened into a horrifying smile as he tightened his grip on Jack's throat, his claws biting deeper. Black, brackish blood trickled down Jack's throat from the punctures.

Jack looked over Grisswell's shoulder at the small red mound lying on the floor. For one brief moment his eyes flashed emerald green, his clawed hand twitched, and in the next instant he was gone through the portal.

"We shall have to acquire a new demon," Emilina said. She turned from the dissipating portal, opened the Book, and placed it on a table next to her. She looked around. The fairy had vanished.

"Where did that little wretch get to?" She scanned the nearby area but as her eyes turned toward the spot where the bag lay, all thoughts of the fairy evaporated. The bag was flat, lying open and empty on the floor.

And next to it stood a very pissed-off Toad.

CHAPTER THIRTY-THREE

**ug had watched** the disturbing movement of the flute as it crawled toward his friend. Though it could never be said that he was a deductive genius, there were times, rare and fleeting, when he did have brushes with inspiration.

He stomped on the flute as hard as he could. For the brief moment that his thick black leather boot was in contact with the instrument, Pug heard Emilina's voice whispering to him. "Come be mine and do as I will."

For that moment he wanted to, more than anything else. And then the flute cracked in two and the thought left his head, nearly as fast as, well, most thoughts left his head. Pug shivered for a moment. When he saw the muddled confusion on Sootfoot's face he grabbed him and dragged him under a low-footed cupboard to keep him safe.

All he knew was that they had to find a better hiding place, and a few moments later a hiding place found him.

≈

The Toad recognized Jack's magic the moment that it had swept over the red velvet bag. She also recognized it for what it truly was: his last attempt to help her.

Jack's spell had been small, so it would go unnoticed. It had done only one simple thing. It had opened the bag and she had hopped out.

She could feel the Form magic surging in herself and she could certainly feel her anger, but there was something else. She felt as if she were standing on the ground in the midst of a lightning storm and she was precisely where the blazing arc of electricity would strike next. But what would it do to her?

Emilina and the Toad glared at each other. Emilina's spiderlike fingers slowly closed into white-knuckled fists as she began to speak.

"Poor Jack. All he ever wanted was to be an artist. Just that one thing," she said. "How terrible for him to meet you, who could be so many things. How unfair. How painful it must have been for him to be your friend. Every moment he knew you must have reminded him of what he could not be. And the only thing he feared came to pass, because of his association with you."

"Shut up," the Toad said as a fire within her began to rage.

"Natterjack is no more because of you."

"I said, SHUT UP!" She was trembling with fury. In her whole life she had never felt such anger. Her eyes went white with it. She hadn't realized that she had attacked Emilina until the moment after it had happened.

She opened her mouth, and her elongated tongue shot through the air. It stretched out impossibly long and struck Emilina solidly in the forehead.

Emilina reached up in shocked surprise and grasped the wet muscle. She twisted and tore at it but it would not come loose.

With a large belching *CRROOOAAAKKK!!!* a blue arcing bolt of electricity shot up the length of the Toad's tongue and slammed into Emilina's head. The force of it blasted the thin woman back against the large oaken doors that led out of the Kitchen. She slid to the ground in a smoldering heap.

The Toad's tongue retracted into her mouth with a quiet *ttthhhhhuuuppp*.

Emilina staggered up, placing her hand on a table for support. The Book lay there within reach. She gave it a lingering glance but didn't pick it up. She turned once again to the Toad.

Emilina's face was burned, a large black scorch mark dead center on her forehead, but already it was growing smaller, her former cadaverous pallor returning as it did. She was not smiling now. Her usual facade of mocking contempt was abandoned.

"You are not the only one here who can call the Deep Magic, child." She raised her long thin fingers, and they began to burn.

Emilina loosed her spell.

Two balls of expanding fire sped toward the Toad. She had just enough time to do the only thing she could do at that moment. She leaped.

Her prodigious leap took her well out of the way of the blast of fire that erupted on the floor, ripping up stone and earth where she had been. Of course, being a panicked Toad, she had not leaped with a particular direction in

mind. And unfortunately, when she struck the floor she did so at the feet of Sarafina.

Sarafina looked down and spoke almost kindly in her deep throaty voice, her mouth still bloody from her fight with Jack. "Wha' a nice jump." And then she kicked the Toad. Hard.

The Toad could not breathe. The force of the kick had taken the wind out of her and sent her tumbling, end over end, back across the floor. She slammed into the side of the cauldron with terrible force. There was a sickening *crack!* and she slid to the floor, her forearm bent at an improbable angle. She did not move.

"Sarafina," Emilina began, "I believe we are pressed for time and need to finish what we have begun. Wouldn't you agree?"

"I do, Sister. I'd like to put this whole mess behind us," Sarafina answered as she spat a glob of blood-stained phlegm on the floor.

"Hand me the Book and let's get on with it."

Sarafina paused for a moment. It was rare that Emilina had ever let her touch the Book, much less that she actually got to look inside at its black, blank pages.

The Book had never liked her.

It had never shown her its secrets or shared any of its arcane recipes but just now as her hand had paused over the Book's black cover she had seen . . . what? A shifting in its surface? An undulation of some sort. It had looked or felt like the Book had taken a breath.

She paused only a second longer, enthralled by the possibility that the Book might finally accept her.

"Today," Emilina prompted in her casually menacing way. If Sarafina had glanced up at her sister she would have seen a look on her face that would have given her pause, but she did not.

Sarafina picked up the Book and the effect was almost instantaneous. She drew a sharp breath.

"Emilina! It's..." Sarafina stood staring at the Book, her face an expression of amazement and greed. "It's speaking to me!"

"Of course it is," Emilina said, and though it was not a pleasing thing to see, she was smiling. It was a cruel smile, but it was genuine, because Emilina was, in all honesty, a cruel person. "You were right, Sarafina."

The large woman's hand trembled slightly as it grasped the shadowed rectangle of black. "I was right? About what?" she asked as she marveled at the hypnotic murmurings and whisperings emanating from the Book.

"About the blood," the thin woman said as she stepped closer to her sister. "It's had a drink and it wants more."

"W...what are you..." Sarafina's eyes grew wide with shock and surprise when she realized what Emilina was talking about.

"I KNEW IT!" she said. "You can't use it. You can't control it anymore because it's had some of your blood. I am right, aren't I, Sister?"

Sarafina held up the Book. In her excitement, she

247

did not notice that its black aura had begun to creep up her hand.

"You are right, Sister, in part. The blood changed things. It awakened the Book's hunger and it will not sleep until it has fed. But . . ." Emilina paused as she watched the black crawl up her sister's arm unnoticed. "It was not my blood spilled on the Book. It was yours."

Sarafina's eyes narrowed and her face twisted into a confused scowl. "What . . . no . . . I wasn't bleeding . . ."

And then she remembered. Her eyes bulged open and her hand shot up to the small bandage on her neck. "The crib! It . . . it . . . pricked me!" The darkness had seeped up Sarafina's arm and began to crawl across her neck and face like writhing tentacles under her skin.

Sarafina tried to release the Book, tried with all her considerable strength to throw it away, but the Book would not let her. No matter how hard she shook her hand it would not permit her to let it go.

She had only enough time to reach for her sister. "Emilina, you put the Book on the table so that I would pick it up . . . on purpose . . . you . . . you . . ." And then her eyes rolled back, exposing only the whites . . . and she was silent.

Emilina watched as the Book infused Sarafina with its steeping shadow.

The large woman was shaking violently. She began sweating a viscous and black fluid and it started to flow like oil down her thick arm into the cover of the Book. There was a nauseating sucking sound that filled the air and Sarafina's form began to drain, to diminish. Her body was liquefying, pouring into the Book with all of her knowledge and powers. It took only moments and . . . she was gone.

Emilina strode over and picked up the Book.

It was pleased. She could sense it. Perhaps it would give her what she wanted. Now that it had eaten.

It was warm in her hands and she could feel its power growing.

She held the Book up high into the dark cold air of the Kitchen. A thickened black tar began to slowly drip out of the cover.

Emilina opened her mouth and began to drink the drips. She could feel Sarafina's magic infusing her, combining with her own. She had fed the Book, and now it was feeding her.

When she finished, she wiped the corners of her mouth primly as someone who had just had a good meal.

And she reached for the unconscious Toad.

CHAPTER THIRTY-FOUR

he first thing the Toad saw when she opened her eyes was a cadaverous pool of green, bubbling bile. She stared at it in confusion.

The open mouth of the cauldron yawned wide beneath her.

Wait. This isn't right. I've already done this once.

The Toad turned and saw the creature that now held her aloft. It was Emilina. And it wasn't.

It looked like Emilina, mostly, with a blackened stain around her mouth, and yet it had some of the facial features of Sarafina and... "Mirabella," the Toad said.

"We may not be natural shape changers, but we manage. Sarafina knew the secrets of combining our powers, and our physical forms as well. Even if she didn't have the mind to know how to make best use of the knowledge. Good witch, bad strategician. When she and I joined to become Mirabella, it was my mind in control. But Sarafina is here," Emilina said. "Right here." The thin woman tapped her own forehead with an index finger that had grown sharp, black, and pointed. "But this time she won't be coming back out."

"NO!" she croaked. "You couldn't!"

"Count yourself lucky, child. If I used the Book rather than the cauldron, your consciousness would become a part of me as well as some of your power. Would you choose to be trapped in my mind for all time?" Emilina smiled, but her eyes were fierce and burning with desire. "Besides, the Book transfers magic, but it consumes so much in the process and leaves little for me. The pot will channel all your abilities to me and, with the pot, you simply die."

"No!" she shouted again.

"Go ahead," Emilina said drily to the toad in her hand. "Use your vulgar magics, your paltry talents."

The Toad did try, but something wasn't right. She couldn't summon her powers. She could feel something fighting against her, trying to muddy her thoughts. She was beginning to feel . . . fragmented and . . . forgetful.

Emilina nodded her head in a satisfied way and held up her other hand. She was holding the Book and waves of pure dark energy pulsed from it.

"I don't have . . . didn't have Sarafina's skill with restraining potions, but I believe this will achieve the proper effect for now," Emilina said. "In a few moments you won't remember you were ever a human at all.

251

"Isn't it interesting," she continued, "we find ourselves back here after everything. Just like we were. Minus a few players, of course, but still. What a huge waste of time this has all been..."

Emilina's grip tightened like a metal vice. She was crushing the wind out of her. The Toad could barely breathe at all and her vision was starting to get hazy around the edges. She was blacking out.

"I...didn't...do...anything," the Toad said between gasps, "but try...to survive."

"And you did," Emilina snarled the words. "As a thorn in my side."

But the Toad didn't reply. She was distracted by a small figure creeping on a nearby sideboard toward Emilina. A figure with two razor-sharp blades in her hands.

It had been a wonder that Horsefly hadn't been crushed or blasted out of existence. During his battle with the Witches, Jack's impish fire had come very close to burning her to a cinder and she had felt the heat of it as it passed over her paralyzed body. She had watched in silence as Grisswell appeared and took Jack away. She had felt the almost imperceptible pulse of the imp's subtle magic when he released the Toad from her containment. Horsefly had hoped that Jack's spell would free her as well but it had not.

But strangely, a moment later, the effects of the flute vanished, and the fairy found herself able to move once again.

Horsefly had been quiet. No, that was an understatement,

she had made no sound whatsoever. After she was released from the flute's spell, she had first stalked the Witches, intending to surprise them with a sneak attack, but the one had consumed the other. The thin one had betrayed her own and Horsefly had watched the wretched scene as it unfolded. After, she had continued her stealthy advance, taking advantage of the fact that the thin Witch's attention was completely focused on the Toad.

Horsefly was almost within striking distance when Emilina turned and screamed.

It was a truly horrifying sound, seeming to contain more than one voice.

Horsefly winced as the foul stench of Emilina's breath washed across her in unbearable waves. She smelled of rancid, rotting meat, candle tallow, and blood.

The thin woman stood, eyes blazing with fury at the fairy. In one hand the Toad gasping for breath, in the other the black Book.

"Interruptions! Always more interruptions!" she screamed. "Perhaps you'd like to be a part of this recipe!"

There was a sound somewhere in the distance of splintering wood, and the fairy dropped into a defensive crouch, blades held high and eyes alert.

Emilina seemed to calm herself and she stood there looking at the fairy with a twisted snarl on her face. "Your knives look sharp," she said, "but let's use mine."

The fairy sensed movement behind and from her left. Though she made a quick lunge to the right she wasn't quick enough. She felt an intense pain as a silver steak knife sliced her shoulder, streaking past her, flying through the air as if thrown.

But it did not fall. As Horsefly watched, it merely circled smoothly in a wide arc and joined what could only be described as a flock of floating blades.

Blood flowed freely from her wound but she didn't notice. All of her attention was focused on the multitude of knives that were hovering above her—all sharp, all pointed at her.

Without warning, a large serrated carving knife struck at her as quick as a snake. She leaped back and the point of the knife dug into the wooden surface of the sideboard. The blade wiggled itself from side to side and slid free of the wood. It rejoined its flock.

"You are a quick little thing. Let's make this challenging, shall we?" Emilina said as the blades began to slowly circle around the fairy.

Horsefly could not escape. The blades circled her, spinning faster and faster, stabbing at her in lightning-quick jabs.

They were large knives compared to her, two or three times her own length, and as she parried one attack after another she realized that they were pushing her closer and closer to the edge of the sideboard.

It seemed that they were just toying with her. They weren't really trying to kill her; they could do that at any moment. But if she fell, she would land in the cauldron, and she knew what that meant: The Witch would steal her magic and leave her a wilted, shriveled husk. If she lived at all.

Another blade thrust at her and she made another parry. One step closer to the edge. Another thrust, another dodge, closer still. All the blades at once, a high leap and she landed a single pace from the edge.

It occurred to her just as defeat seemed inevitable. The blades didn't have minds of their own; it was the Witch's mind controlling them.

As the Kitchen knives closed in upon her for the last time she turned, and with all her strength she threw both of her swords.

CHAPTER THIRTY-FIVE

AAARRRRREEEIIIGGHHHH!"

Emilina's piercing scream echoed in the Kitchen and was answered from all directions by wicked creatures joining their voices to the sound, like a pack of howling wolves.

But this time in her scream, in addition to the anger, there was pain.

Horsefly's swords had flown straight and true. They were wings, after all, and infused with her own powerful binding magic.

One blade pierced Emilina's right wrist and, as her hand spasmed in pain, she dropped the Toad. The other blade pierced her left wrist, which would have caused her to drop the Book, if the Book would have permitted itself to be dropped.

"I DON'T HAVE TIME FOR THIS!" Emilina screeched as she twisted her right hand up into a claw and threw a ball of blue-green fire at the fairy.

Horsefly lunged to her left, but the crackling ball of magic exploded under her feet and sent her catapulting into the air. Though she tried to roll with the impact, she still smashed to the tabletop with terrific force.

Emilina threw another bolt at the stunned fairy, who was struggling to her feet—an easy target.

The Toad leaped to the edge of the table and snagged the fairy with her sticky, elongated tongue. She pulled her out of the way at the last possible moment, the ball of energy blasting a hole in the table. The Toad and the fairy stood leaning against each other.

Emilina snarled a deep, rattling growl that sounded more as if it were coming from a rabid beast than a person. She opened her mouth and a black stinking fog poured out, twisting in and out of the shelves and dishes and aged stone of the room itself.

The Witch tilted her head back and stretched her hands out to the darkness of the Kitchen and the Book pulsed a solid wave of magic that rippled and spread out in all directions. Every creature that lived in the Kitchen felt a shuddering despair as it passed through them. She sent her magic into the blackest corners and drew to herself all of the power that resided there. There were sounds of breaking glass and groaning wood and rending metal. The

foul shadows that answered Emilina's summoning rippled through the very stone of the floor and made it buck and heave. The nearby cabinets and shelves began to warp and writhe and change as the dark tendrils wove themselves into the wood, metal, and glass of the furnishings. Utensils, bottles, dishes, and the hinged doors that hung on the cabinets began to shake ferociously.

There was scratching and clawing and snapping as a nearby chair broke itself and reformed into a clutching, crawling spindle-legged beast. It was still a chair, yes, but now it had a mouth full of splintered, ragged teeth and multijointed legs that ended in sharpened stakes. It began circling the sideboard where the fairy and the Toad stood leaning against each other. It crept like a spider and it was not alone.

The knives that had crashed to the floor suddenly flung themselves together in a cluster and bits and pieces melted and flowed together until it was a single thing. A crawling, slicing thing that drew deep gouges in the very stone that it skittered upon.

Emilina plucked Horsefly's blade from her left wrist. She spoke a single word. The fairy screamed and dropped to her knees as the sword burst into a small cloud of ash.

"NO!" the Toad shouted but her voice was lost in the clawing of tables, the scraping of chairs, and the movements of hideous things.

Horsefly lurched at Emilina but the Toad held her back.

The creatures that were crawling and clutching around them would have her in an instant if she leaped off the sideboard. There were just too many. And if that weren't enough, the crines appeared, too, holding their distance and not wanting to get swept up in the maelstrom. They were waiting for their chance.

The Witch lifted her right wrist to her mouth and extracted the second blade with her teeth. She took it in her hand and held it out so that the fairy could see it plainly, and a moment later it too was gone.

The Fairy shuddered and fell limp, a dead weight in the Toad's arms. She let Horsefly slide gently to the sideboard's surface and stood over her to shield her from the encroaching chaos.

At least my head has cleared, she thought. Even as she had the thought, she found magic was rising in her as well. It seemed a small comfort in the face of what she now witnessed.

Wooden and metal conglomerations yawned and snapped at them from all angles. Jagged dishes spun and flew and dashed themselves to shards as they hurled themselves at the Toad and her fallen friend.

The Toad faced the nearest threat, a collection of broken glass that had transformed into a crablike monstrosity. It scuttled toward her, claws snapping, pincers opening and closing.

She clutched at the fairy, dragging her back away from

the creature. She looked all around but there was nowhere left to run.

Suddenly, as she glanced back at the crab thing, an image flickered briefly in her vision. For a moment she saw not what the thing was, not what it had become, but what it was supposed to be, what it should have been, not unlike her vision of Horsefly when she had returned her sword.

"Crroooakkk..." A small wave of blue energy sprang from her mouth and instantly the creature of glass changed. The jagged crystalline nightmare twirled and reformed into a smooth, longneck glass bottle. It rocked gently to a stop and sat motionless on the table.

The chair spider leaped and jarred the table, sending the bottle crashing to the floor, where the glass fragments lay unmoving.

The Toad turned, croaked again, and in the next moment a rather normal dining chair landed next to the small pile of broken glass.

The Toad spun and croaked as creature after creature raced forward to consume her. Each time she did a table or a kettle, a pot or a pan, crashed to the floor, reverting back to its original shape.

The knife creature launched itself into the air and hurtled at the Toad.

Her croak struck the creature in midair and it reverted as the others had done but...

Crud, she thought as she scooped up the fairy and

made a stumbling lunge backward, toward the edge of the tabletop.

The knives, though no longer enchanted, rained down, clanking and embedding themselves in the spot where she and Horsefly had been.

The Toad and the fairy fell roughly and nearly slid right off the edge. She looked down. The red velvet bag, now with a life of its own, was crawling back and forth on the floor, waiting for her to fall so that it could swallow her once again.

"No you don't," she said as she stood and pulled the fairy away from the precipice.

Emilina turned and with a wave of her hand the mish-mash of nightmare creatures parted and stepped aside, creating a path leading deep into the Kitchen and growing strangely quiet like an expectant crowd at an execution. They revealed an immense figure. The large shape seemed to brood in its own flickering light. It did not move, at first.

Emilina held up the Book and a bolt of dark lightning arced to the massive black form. It immediately began to shudder. The cauldron, which had been stationed at Emilina's side, began to back away.

The floor that surrounded the thing told its age. The stones where it squatted were blackened with soot and cracked from centuries of bearing its enormous weight. The whole area was burned and charred.

It was as round as a column, and thicker than Sarafina had been, but it was not human, or animal for that matter, not in any way. Large gouts of red and orange flame suddenly spewed from its midsection through heavy iron grating, and as it exhaled thick grey clouds of smoke, it began to shift from side to side. The sounds of cracking stone and the groan of metal filled the silence. It was pulling itself out of the ancient stone floor. Three immense iron legs pulled out of where they had been embedded in stone and began stepping toward her, the ground shaking with every step.

"Every kitchen has a stove," Emilina said with malignant humor. "Burnard hasn't cooked anything in a very long time. I wouldn't want him to feel left out of this dish."

The pot-bellied beast began to plod forward and the Toad saw that it had three thick stovepipes that reached up into the air spewing noxious fumes. The pipes began to move and writhe like huge tentacles. An aged cupboard scurried to avoid the oncoming behemoth but when it did not move fast enough the oven struck out with terrifying force. One of the long thick stovepipes smashed through the cupboard and it exploded in a shower of splintered wood. The other denizens scrambled away from the fearsome brute. The cauldron huddled, shivering, behind Emilina.

The stone floor cracked with each step Burnard took. It sounded like the breaking of bone.

The Toad was terrified. She croaked a pulse of magic

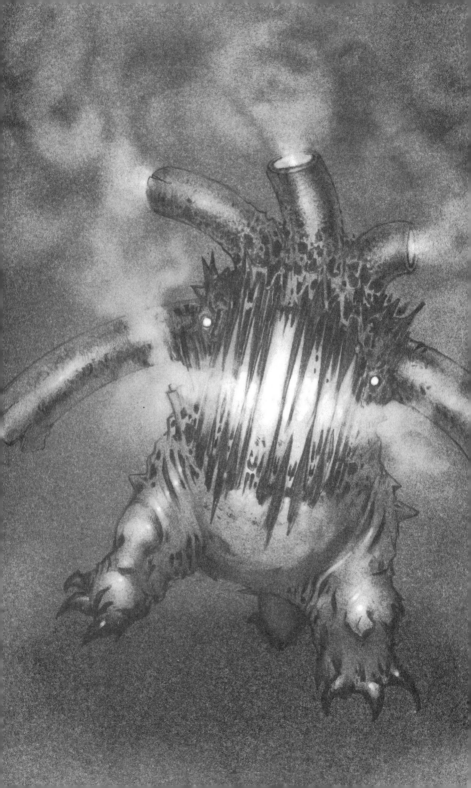

at the cast-iron monster. Where it struck, its metal shifted like the dim prismatic sheen of black oil but otherwise it did not slow the creature, not even a little.

And it was closer now. She could feel the heat of the raging fire within its vast, vented belly. It was rapidly becoming unbearable.

The Toad's colors began to shift; she took an absolutely huge breath and she erupted in an enormous, *"CRRRR-ROOOOOOAAAAAAKKKKK!"*

The blast struck the oven dead center. It seemed to totter for a moment but, as the Toad watched, Emilina sent another arc of negative lightning and the beast, reenergized, continued to advance.

It was almost upon her. In moments the huge crushing stovepipes would be crashing down on the sideboard. The Toad was near fainting from the exhaustion of channeling so much magic. There was nowhere to run. She and the Horsefly would be pulverized. It would be over and they would be dead.

"At least she won't have me," the Toad said to herself. She readied herself for one final desperate attempt, but paused as Horsefly's thin, melodic voice whispered up to her from the table. "Do not attack the weapon; attack the wielder," she said and then went silent.

The Toad watched as all three immense iron appendages raised high in the air to deliver the killing blow, her skin stinging from the intense heat in the belly of Burnard. She picked up the fairy and threw her to the opposite side

of the table to get her out of harm's way. Horsefly flew through the air. Unconscious, she landed and, as limp as a rag doll, slid off the edge of the table, out of sight.

Toad turned just in time to see the bludgeoning, smoking pipes begin their descent. She had barely enough time to gather herself for one final effort. In the scant moment before she, and most likely the sideboard, were crushed into oblivion, she made a tremendous leap.

Straight at Emilina.

As she leaped, she changed. It would have been poetic or at least poetic justice if she had transformed into a beautiful, fierce falcon, but she did not. Nor did she become human; she did not yet know how. She did change, though, like most of the magic that the Toad had used, it was a physical representation of her emotions. Right now those emotions were feral, almost primal expressions of fear and rage.

She landed with a solid *THWACK* squarely on Emilina's face, and the Toad that was no longer a toad was barely conscious of the fact that she had transformed at all. It was a grey-green leaper that leaped through the air, but the creature that had collided with Emilina's face was leathery and brown, muscular and toothy. In a rumbling growl, she said, "YOU WANT A PIECE OF ME, WITCH? HOW 'BOUT I TAKE A PIECE OF YOU INSTEAD!"

Emilina stood stunned in momentary disbelief. The Toad, who was now an ig-troll, opened her muscled jaws and sank her fangs deep into Emilina's pointed nose. She shrieked as the batlike creature tore off a considerable chunk of flesh and spat it out. Her hands jerked up, snatching at the troll, but she was gone. She'd sprung away, lightning quick, and glided toward the floor, transforming into the Toad once more.

Before she landed, she had time to see the open mouth of the red velvet bag beneath her. She filled with dread.

Emilina clutched at her nose as the blood ran between her fingers, but she was also smiling. She watched the wretched Toad fall into the confinement bag.

"Finally, we can be done," she said as she took a step forward.

As it turned out, she was right.

It was a small thing, really. It had no magic, at least very little. A tiny black marble that no one would have noticed. It would have been lost in the Kitchen forever, if Emilina hadn't stepped on it. If it hadn't caused her to slip and stumble backward. If the back of her knees hadn't struck hot metal.

Emilina, arms flailing wildly, spun out of balance and fell headfirst into the cauldron.

The world went white.

Or so it seemed. Magic exploded from the cauldron.

The sides of the ancient metal pot ruptured and blew out with tremendous force in all directions, and with it, a hurricane of magical energies.

It was a white-hot torrent of magic channeled from the deepest places of the Kitchen coupled with the Book, and

Emilina, and all the energies that they had usurped and consumed in their long existence. It exploded out, swirled around in eddies, and crashed like white water; and the bag was caught up and carried like a child's toy in a flash flood.

Sarafina had constructed the bag and its magic well. It shielded the Toad from the energies of the explosion, but her physical body was being buffeted and bruised.

Just before she felt the last fragment of her mind slip into unconsciousness, she reached out with her hand, and found something. It grew warm in her palm.

She could not see it with her eyes, she couldn't see anything in the absolute black of the bag, but she knew what it was. She could feel the smooth carved stone still draped around her neck with the fairy braid. She held it tight against her chest.

An image flashed in her thoughts.

A carving of a girl, a young woman, rough-hewn, vague as if seen through the veil of a dream. She focused her thoughts and the image clarified and came into sharp focus.

Her name is Katherine ... my name is Katherine.

And suddenly everything changed.

CHAPTER THIRTY-SIX

The young woman stood in a sunlit kitchen, a normal kitchen, looking down at a small stone carving of a toad in her hand. Jack's carving. There had been something in it after all. It had been her.

There was no sign of Emilina or anything else from the dark Kitchen except on the floor: a crumpled red cloth. The bag, its magic expended, had not survived Katherine's transformation.

There were rusted shards of an old black kettle strewn among the dust and debris littered about the floor. It looked as if it had been in pieces for an age. The room looked long forgotten and unused, as if it had been unlived in and exposed to the elements for a very long time.

The doors of this kitchen were open, but not to a

darkened, candlelit hallway. There was nothing outside these doors but a cobblestone path, surrounded by green grass, tall swaying trees, and a sky that seemed too big, too bright, and too blue.

She felt a strange calm, as if she had just woken from a long sleep. After what seemed so long a time in the dark, not knowing, not being who she really was, to suddenly find herself standing in the warm dappled light of the sun as it shone through the trees, and into the windows of this old cottage kitchen, was almost unbelievable. She stood waiting for something to happen. There were no sounds but the rustling of the wind.

Her eyes caught a glimpse of movement. In the bright light of day Horsefly looked like a wisp of smoke, but she was there, and when she found a small shadow under a table she grew a little more solid.

"Are you all right?"

The fairy looked up at her weakly, shrugged, and said in her melodic voice, "I may be."

Katherine sensed another presence. Two, actually.

"Pug...Sootfoot, where are you?"

From under the mangled pieces of the red velvet bag, Sootfoot was forcefully pushed and he stumbled to the floor, his flute broken in half. He clutched the pieces to his chest.

Pug, who had pushed him, stepped out a moment later.

"How did you make it out?" she asked.

"Well," Pug started, "I followed on Jack's heels but

when I came through, um...things were a bit messy. I saw Sootie here tryin' ta use his flute on Jack. Ya see, ol' Broomhead had the thing magiked so that anyone who was usin' it was under her power. That's how they found us out, and what we was up to...so I broke it. Soot and I figured to stay hidden. The Kitchen went kerflooey and all that mess with the stove started up. That blasted sack crept up on us and gulped us down. A few moments later it scooped up the fairy but she was out like a light. We heard the Witch start her screeching and the next thing we knew it'd swallered you, too. Say"—he paused—"yer a bit taller now and much less...warty," he said, looking up at her. When she was a toad he had been taller than her but now at her true size and shape he could have easily stood on her palm.

"I didn't know you were in the sack," she said.

"Well, there was a lot goin' on, now weren't there?" Pug said and, suddenly frowning, added, "Say...is the Kitchen gone? I mean, is it destroyed? 'Cause I had family in there. I ain't seen most of 'em in a while, but still..."

Katherine shook her head. "No. Jack said the Kitchen was an entire world that bumped up next to ours. It's all still there. I can feel it. The connection has been broken, that's all."

"Seems enough," Pug said.

Her attention turned to Sootfoot. Katherine looked at him for a moment and saw him for what he truly was...

She reached down to him and put her hand lightly on his head. He turned from her.

"I...I didn't mean..." he started to say, but he would not meet her eyes.

"I know. It doesn't matter, Soot. It wasn't your fault," she said softly. "It really wasn't. I still would like to think of you as my friend, if you'll let me."

He gazed gratefully at her. "I wish..." he started to say, but Katherine interrupted.

"Don't wish. Just tell me what you want."

Sootfoot looked at her; there was shame and sadness in his eyes.

"I just want to run in the forest. Sometimes I dream of running and it feels simple and free. It feels like a memory"—he paused—"but I've been in the dark so long."

"Shhh," she said as she stroked the soft fur of his head once, twice, and on the third touch a small snow white fox with black feet looked up at her. It sniffed her hand, grew timid, and sprinted to the open door. It paused for a moment, looking back, as a soft breeze from the outside world blew through its fur, and then it was gone, running out of sight.

"Um...yer not gonna turn me inta nuthin,' are ya?" Pug said, smiling, but still a little concerned.

She returned his smile. "I gave him what he wanted. I made him what he should have been."

Looking up she saw something lying on the tabletop, the only tabletop in the room.

She reached out and picked up the Book and turned it over in her hands. Nothing odd or strange happened. She looked at the cover. It was simple, worn brown leather with one word embossed.

She read it aloud:

"Beneath."

She opened the Book and looked at the first page. The author's name was Mortimer Thyme. She flipped a page or two and read: RECIPE FOR UNDONE BUN, INGREDIENTS: 3 OF HEARTS, A CROW'S FOOT, AND A SIMPLE NELSON.

What's a simple nelson? She paused as it dawned on her.

This isn't truth, she thought plainly.

Katherine closed the Book and placed it on the table in front of her. She laid her hand flat on the Book and said, "This is not the truth. Show me your face."

Under her hand the Book began to smolder and sizzle. The brown cover seemed to char instantly into black. She lifted her hand and saw a symbol where the title should have been. It was a black-on-black star, beneath a black-on-black sun.

She stared at the symbol and thought:

Now tell me what it means.

As she stared at this strange pictogram, its meanings flooded into her mind. She sensed that it was a word from a language older perhaps than her world. It was sophisticated and twisted and of many duplicitous meanings. The knowledge of it in her mind felt malevolent, felt like insanity...and it had a voice. It began to offer her things. "I am yours now. Be mine and I will give you everything that you desire."

Katherine began to breathe shallow and fast, her face becoming strained and pale.

Suddenly, she slapped her hand on the cover of the Book.

"STOP!" she shouted.

Immediately the Book was silent; the thoughts dissipated and the whirling, spinning motions inside her head vanished. She rocked back on her heels with a slight feeling of vertigo.

The Book was just a book once more.

She stepped back from the table and held her hand palm-down toward the floor. A finger-length shard of iron from the shattered kettle wriggled and rose to her.

This will do. It's good...and strong... She thought of Jack, of his hands.

She held up her other hand and a large wooden block moved from the corner of the room and elongated, changing shape into a rough stonecutter's mallet.

It took a great deal of effort and focus to effect the change. Her battle in the Kitchen, her transformation, returning Sootfoot to his natural form, had taken a lot out of her. She felt drained but still, she had to do this last thing.

She stepped to the table and placed the shard on the center of the Book and without hesitation she swung the mallet up and then down, driving it through the Book into the table beneath.

The Book did not scream or bleed or change in any way...but she was pleased. The iron would hold its magic fast, for a while, at least.

She could sense the dark Kitchen. It was still very near and the power that linked that world to this one was still here as well. Weak now, but it would build again.

"Come on, you two. Let's get going. I want to find my way home."

She stepped over to the doorsill and paused looking down at the threshold. In the corner of the doorjamb a glint caught her eye. She reached down and picked up the small blackstone marble. There was a hairline crack that ran through its center.

"You're free, Bibbett," she said quietly, "and so am I."

She tucked the marble into her pocket and stepped through the door.

She walked to the edge of the forest and found the beginning of a path. Pug sat on her shoulder and in her hand she cradled Horsefly. The little fairy was as ethereal and insubstantial as a hot breath on a cold day, but though she had lost her swords, she carried on. Perhaps she would survive after all. Katherine looked back at the modest keep and cottage.

She stepped onto the path. The journey would probably be long and night would come soon but she was not afraid.

She had, after all, become accustomed to the dark.